The Gnome Stories

The Gnome Stories

ANDER MONSON

Graywolf Press

This publication is made possible, in part, by the voters of Minnesota through a
Minnesota State Arts Board Operating Support grant, thanks to a legislative
appropriation from the arts and cultural heritage fund. Significant support has
also been provided by Target, the McKnight Foundation, the Lannan Foundation,
the Amazon Literary Partnership, and other generous contributions from foundations, corporations, and individuals. To these organizations and individuals we
offer our heartfelt thanks.

Published by Graywolf Press
250 Third Avenue North, Suite 600
Minneapolis, Minnesota 55401

www.graywolfpress.org

Published in the United States of America

ISBN 978-1-64445-012-3

2 4 6 8 9 7 5 3 1
First Graywolf Printing, 2020

Library of Congress Control Number: 2019933471

Cover design: Walter Green

For Megan

Contents

The
Gnome
Stories

Weep No More Over This Event

I came upon him as he was rustling through the DVDs, throwing them into a sack in what appeared to be a self-congratulatory way, laughing to himself, probably at the selection, which was my wife's, and I was doubly enraged. I don't know why I thought of it when action was required, but I wondered where people got sacks like this, as in could you buy them at the supermarket, or were these specialized burglary tools endorsed by criminals? I was standing on the steps coming down from the spacious landing to the main floor, and I wondered also how he got through the alarm system I had installed after my wife saw too many of those threatening commercials on television and I felt the pressure of my husbandness coming down on me, and I called and got jacked by the small print but had it installed nevertheless, which gesture did not stop my wife from leaving.

I found out after she left that you can set the system, which is admittedly pretty glorious, to keep someone from leaving the house, too, though I did not read the entire instruction manual at the time and it would only seem important to me later, like most realizations I have had in my life.

So I was watching and he must have heard me coming down or something because he turned to me, and it must have been hard to see me in the dark because he began to walk toward me. That's why I shot him. He advanced on me. He was an imminent threat. This is what the police told me later as I sobbed, more for the loss of my marriage than any kind of ruined innocence.

The fat policeman explained it like this: To shoot him where he stands is allowed now by law in this state, and is more than allowed, is in fact requisite of the situation, which is to say that you did the right thing and should weep no more over this event.

I liked that he said weep no more, like this was all a tragedy or a musical or spiritual. He asked if anything was missing, if this had occurred before, seeing the new alarm system on the wall and its array of lights blinking into a new configuration. I told him no, not as far as I could tell without inventorying the entire house, and no, it hadn't ever happened before. Then I told him about the commercials.

Mm-hm, he said, I've seen those too. It's good you had it, because it shows a lack of premeditation on your part, not that it matters since he was in your house, dude. He might have said *sir* instead of *dude*, but it's hard to remember the exactitude of language in moments like these.

I said I found the pattern of the lights to be beautiful. He stared at me and did not blink until I spoke again.

I explained about my wife. How she had left a month ago and I think he divined the implied emptiness because he had a ring still on his finger. He looked at me like he was thinking of his own wife in this moment. He took down my information, took me to the station to give my statement, said it would only take an hour and then I could come back to my domicile and lie down, watch some news, or whatever I needed to do to get it off my mind.

The event weighed on me, though not in the way I expected. I was in the middle of a department store floor contemplating a couple of blow-up Christmas decorations to add to my menagerie, when I had what I guess you could call a flashback, or maybe a portent, or just a dream. In it my wife and I were in bed, and we had been crying separately for an hour, and had just drifted off to sleep, when I heard someone downstairs and so I got the gun and went downstairs and there he was, and I was on the stairs with my wife's presence behind me, like I was guarding her from him, and when I shot him all I could see was light, and then she was gone, and it's true, she is gone, she had gone, gone some time ago, and all I had left was light, and the house, her DVDs, and the system, and my menagerie.

Men of a certain age begin accumulation of collections. Some are private, like my father's collection of over six thousand toy rocket ships. He had two whole rooms devoted to them. This was when I was a teenager, before I left that house, after Mom had died, after it had seemed so empty for a couple years, and he had started to fill it up with this stuff. I was a teenager then and wanted to blow the rockets up, but didn't because I feared his anger. I still fear his anger, really. When I called him to tell him I shot a man and should weep no more about it, since he was in my house, since he was advancing on me, Dad told me it was okay. He had shot a man in wartime but never talked about it. We waited on the phone, neither of us saying much of anything, which was how most of our conversations went. I had expected him to have some wisdom for me, but he never was much for wisdom. He said, you sound lonely, son. You should get a cat. I told him I would think about it. He said go to shoot for a while at the target range. Sometimes others will come to a house once it's been broken into, even when you shot the guy. You should be careful. You have all that Christmas shit to protect. He was joking, but it was true.

My collection is on my lawn, all over the exterior of my house. I tell myself it's for the kids, the families in the neighborhood. My neighbor, Rutan, has a competing collection. His display is spectacular. He has twice the inflatable Christmas decorations, even makes stuff by hand. There are lights and moving parts. I got the idea from him. When Katie and I would come back at night and go by that house with all those inflatable things alive, the air compressor humming, with them moving back and forth in the night, it impressed me. You could see it from our bedroom window. I could see it as we fucked. I could see it after. It was like I was fucking Santa, the reindeer, a series of penguins, Dora the Explorer. It glowed all night. Sometimes it was all I'd look at. Now I have my own. Rutan was a single guy. I think for him it was a little desperate; he was into Christmas, sure, but he didn't have any kids, no wife. I think he was trying to attract them by accumulating the trappings of Christmas cheer. He and I are making our own society here—people came from across the whole city after they read an article about us in the paper. He spent most evenings outside, adjusting the compressors and the angles, talking to the gawkers, suggesting photos, giving hugs. It is not impossible that his method will work.

Here's the problem: my domicile immediately began to appeal to me less—it felt like a mausoleum, or, maybe, not that, a crime scene, then. A place where I couldn't forget the past. If someone could be shot there, if I could be home invaded and, potentially, if she were still here, Katie could have been carried off and raped, or traumatized because of this, then it was a problem—my problem, this city's problem, America's problem—but I was the only one able to take action. I had already taken action. What I needed was I needed more action.

I couldn't stop thinking about it, like the way I thought about my mother at unexpected times and couldn't get her out of my head, like when Katie and I were having sex one of the many times we called our first for effect, and she was high, but I wasn't, and she was talking about the thousand needles all around us, by which I take it she meant the stars. I did not tell her about my mother's face hovering above me because women don't want that kind of honesty, no matter what they say.

Some nights I would sit at my own darkened window and watch the lights wink off in the neighbors' windows, or what I could see of them through the trees. I'd see silhouettes, a setting sun of motion in a window. I felt increasingly sure that eyes were looking back at me. So I installed a more robust security system with encrypted codes and a superspectrum something or other that transmits signals to itself and its backup systems via infrared. This may have been about sexual jealousy, but I don't like to think about that very much.

Of course at first I tried some spells that I found on the internet, but they had no effect at all. I don't know what I expected but it was worth a shot and I thought back to days playing D&D with friends in high school and how magic was one option, and Katie had gone and we had said some things, and it had been weeks by this point, and I wasn't sure where she was—she'd said just don't fucking call her for a while, that she had things to work out, probably in Cancún. So I had the alarm system—a kind of spell of protection—installed and I lit some candles for the incantation, too many as it turned out, since it set off the fire alarm, which triggered a manned response by the security team—this is why I signed up for them, the personal responses, the sense that we, that I, have a security team ready for response at the slightest electronic dip or tuck or wavering—and I had to call them off and tell them the code word and all that.

They do a good job with all of this. Like in the commercials, they make the effort to make it realistic for you. I was charmed. I felt completed. And happy that I purchased the second gun they recommended after the invasion: a .357 pistol, big and loud and hard, an exclamation point in my hands. My forearm holds the memory of firing at the range, shot after shot, meaning something probably in Morse code, followed by muscle soreness, which wasn't much different from firing at the guy on the carpet in the main room, the intruder, the interloper in my domicile, attempting to make off with my—with Katie's—probably ridiculous shit.

I don't know what exactly I'm trying to tell you here, why this is emerging the way it is, what secret I have to offer up that you might be amazed by. I look down and see a spider slowly skittering up to me. I hold my ground. I will live in peace with it, even if I am terrified of them. It will spin its threads and capture interlopers and slowly consume them: Nature's Defense. It disappears. See. I can coexist with something. This is already helping.

The more I contemplated possible entrances into the house—the twin skylights upstairs, the chimneys, the forty windows—the more I became convinced I would have to try out each of them. The security system wasn't wired to the skylights yet, you see, because I hadn't asked and I hadn't thought it realistic to deal with that. I purchased some burglar's tools on the internet including the cool suction cup thing that you attach to glass and cut out a circle and it doesn't fall in, waking whoever's inside. I tried it on the window. It took longer than I thought it would but it went eventually: with practice I could take out a pane of glass in a minute, I thought. I added this to the list of Additional Skills that I liked to deploy to impress Katie or possible employers. She'd be excited when I demonstrated some of these.

I could see Rutan's lights just past my lights outside. I thought it important to appeal to passersby. The lights, I realize now, may have been a defense mechanism of another sort. They warmed the exterior of the house. They warmed my heart. They warmed a thousand visitors' hearts inside their bodies as they drove by with their families' bodies and their eyes adjusting to our sudden light explosions.

I didn't take the guy's mask off. When the cops showed up they shooed me out of the house so I didn't have to see his face. Maybe they thought that would make a difference in terms of my psychological recovery time. The fat and sensitive cop gave me a couple of cards for psychologists to talk to after an event like this. They said to be careful upon waking— and to unload the gun for a couple weeks. People sometimes went a little nuts after.

I admit I couldn't sleep. Not before, even, really, but certainly not now. Part of that was Katie's fault: she'd want to sleep on me, like it gave her peace to be warmed from underneath, which was fine as far as it went, but I got hot too fast and would have to eject her for a while, and then she would get cold, and we would repeat. Sometimes it led to sex, which was better than the other times.

I began to think of myself less as a person and more as a force. I was becoming a force of vengeance, of redemption, a force of comeuppance for those who broke into homes and tried to make off with loot, who made off with our neighbors' daughters, who left no trace at all behind.

A month later, I broke into my first house. It's hard to explain why. I don't even think I know. I made sure no one was home, casing it for a couple days. Chose a neighbor, Danny, whose wife had died two years ago. His daughter had also disappeared. I'd gone to his wife's funeral and not known what to say. And in any of our subsequent interactions, I still didn't know. I considered this a failure, as we had briefly bonded over discussions of the World Cup soccer matches just before his wife passed, and what we had—which wasn't much surely, but it was something—has collapsed.

But being in his house (he had no security system) in his absence was exhilarating. I did not bring my gun. I didn't plan on taking anything. I just wanted to be out of my space for a while, in somebody else's. It had been a while since I had last been inside his house. Katie and I had attended a Super Bowl party a year ago, a sea of awkwardness, not just because I knew how much she hated football but also because I'd talked her into it, feeling like we had to go just to break up the sea of dudes. I had said we really ought to go, and she wouldn't be the only woman there, which turned out not to be true, and she had left one quarter and four beers in, and had not returned, in spite of the hospitality, which was impressive, considering Danny had to learn to do a lot of things for himself after his wife died, and so every occasion was an occasion for him to commit a major social error. I knew he thought about these occasions for error because he often joked about it after he had a couple of drinks, him knowing that I was interested in systems and constantly trying to figure out what to do or say in any situation. I had felt torn between these two obligations: a sort of approximation of maleness, what he and I were supposed to be able to do together, and my love for Katie, who had no love for football or Danny, and no pity for his predicament, this particular brand of loneliness, the still-empty room he had kept that way, just as it was, for his daughter if she ever came back, if anyone ever found her, or if what happened to her became apparent, like if the body was found. I felt we could cut him a little bit of slack considering. Katie had said before that he was a clueless dick, and losing his wife didn't make him any less of one, though I argued that it gave him complexity, and she said well then he is a complex clueless dick, which even I had to admit was true, though the complexity itself was an achievement, I said, something to aspire to. This was our problem, she said later, after I stayed for the rest of the game, my inability to commit to her needs at the expense of society's, and she said it like that, that my connection with Danny was just a social obligation. I said what is our connection then, and that didn't go well at all. Marriage is a social institution as is a neighborhood, and both come with obligations: the lawn, the trash, the lights, the packages we give each other because of grief a couple times a year, or because of fear of loss or change, keeping up the appearance of the exterior of the house, attending events you have no interest in, and my list went on for a while, ever increasing the more I thought about it. The point I was trying to make was that we were both part of something besides ourselves. She may have agreed, but she wanted finally to be ranked higher in one of the many lists I made of My Priorities in order to keep myself on task, make sure I met all the obligations I had committed to.

Sure, yeah, I trawled through his stuff. I had held myself back for so long it felt like freedom. I went in his daughter's room and sat on the bed, tried to envision her, to imagine the last time she was in there. It wasn't untouched—it was clean but still recognizable as the room of a fourteen-year-old. I don't know how to describe it except to say you could feel the past there.

Shortly after the shooting I added Assess Self for Post-Traumatic Stress Disorder to the list of priorities. The literature said this was often an aftereffect of a shooting, that the experience would persist in a halo of related symptoms. I wondered if burglary could be a direct result of that, if crime could perpetuate itself in this way and continue spreading out into a matrix in the world, and if so, maybe that was the reason why the guy was ransacking Katie's DVD collection and I was in the middle of Danny's living room with all the furniture circled like a fortress with several televisions at the center. Danny'd acquired something like a dozen cats since his wife's death, which probably meant something in terms of his psychology, and they moved around my feet—half hopefully, half in warning—as I padded around the carpet, inspecting his DVD collection, which included what appeared to be a complete set of Emmanuelle films. Interesting. They might have been his wife's, or perhaps he bought them as a tribute to his wife, who looked, before the chemo, more than a little like Sylvia Kristel, the star of the majority of them.

I slid one in and turned it on. I looked at the photos of the two of them and their daughter on the wall. I looked at the screen. It was a little like watching a ghost. A sexy ghost.

Obviously I didn't get through more than a half hour of the film without resorting to masturbation. I admit it. It was not my house, not my DVDs, not echoes of my dead wife. It was barely even my body by the time I finished and hit eject, ashamed, though I wasn't yet sure why, then powered off. Then the house was dark and his little girl was still vanished, his wife was still dead. The cats were everywhere.

Headlights started to pass the house and soon it was regular, a metronome. Where does this sudden traffic come from? Could it be police? Could I be surrounded? What I feared was not the consequences but the confrontation, that Danny might come home unexpectedly, that Danny would see me here among his everything that is no longer either his or everything, since I am here and his wife is not, and he would shoot me down, imminent threat, as I stood to go toward him, to shake his hand or offer explanation, as society would deem appropriate. I would make it easier for him, I think, even now. Another pair of headlights passed through the windowshades but did not approach. I could tell him he really should get one of the security systems filled with lights. For the memory of Marie, his wife, I thought of her name just now in this equilibrium we can call a developing situation in my mind if not in the real room here in front of me. I could go, I realized, or I could stay and wait for him. But what would really happen is something unexpected. Maybe the cat-sitter shows up and dies of fright, or a plane drops from the sky through this roof and takes me down in flames. Or he could never return: maybe he left for good, abandoned it, what remained of his life, or maybe he was on that plane. Maybe he was dead in one of the rooms of the house and his life had eroded to the point that he would lie undiscovered here for four days, no one here to check on him, flesh torn off in tiny bits by cats, only to be found by his masturbating home-invading neighbor, himself the victim of a home invasion, and the beginning of a wave of them, every home invasion leading to another.

But nothing happened. Everything collided in my mind and there were cats swirling through the darkness. Katie would disapprove. She hadn't even called to harass me, which means she cares even less than I would have thought. It is unfortunate. I am singularly unfortunate. But I had power. I have power. I have a gun. I shot that man down and continue to do so every night. I came all over the DVD case of *Emmanuelle in Space* thinking about a dead woman and had to clean it up. This is a personal low for me, I thought at the time, though I don't think that anymore. I've since surpassed it.

I cleaned up, got up, and left his space. I did a couple of dishes, which seemed appropriate. I felt just a little smaller after, like I had reduced myself in some barely noticeable way, but mostly I felt new. Maybe this was post-traumatic stress disorder, where you go a little crazy later and start masturbating in your neighbors' houses? I reasoned my behavior could easily be explained in terms of biological irregularity in the brain.

The worst part for Danny was when his daughter had been gone for a week—her name was Marie, too, but she wanted to be called Mary in the way that kids want to differentiate themselves from everything they dislike about the world—and speculation in the neighborhood began to turn on Danny and Marie. We didn't want to speculate about the rest of us. None of us could be responsible. We couldn't even start to think it. We were all responsible adults with cars and cats and curs yowling through the nights, proclaiming their alarm at our perversities. The police weren't releasing any new news. No leads. The parents were naturally persons of interest in the investigation, but nothing was disclosed to connect them to her vanishing. Statistics we saw on TV said that, in seventy-five percent of missing persons cases, the one responsible is a family member or someone who knows the girl well. But the woman on the television said that Danny and Marie were surely beyond reproach. And you could see it in the shot of them on camera as Marie delivered her tearful plea. It was moving, it really was. It could have been any of our daughters if we had daughters, that lovely trouble. Their faces were drawn like their window shades. The two of them had taken to living in near-darkness, and left the house as undisturbed as was possible while still living in it just in case there was some kind of useful evidence not yet identified by the authorities.

This was five years ago. As soon as Mary disappeared my wife started her conjecture, throwing out theories, identifying creepy people we had encountered, even wondering privately about the perverts in our neighborhood who she claimed would follow girls around, to stores, and with cameras in their shopping bags, trying to take photos up their skirts and post them on the internet. She'd seen it happen a couple times, and had heard about it even more. She had this theory that the more leisure time our neighbors had, and let's face it, we lived in a neighborhood that bespoke nothing if not leisure, the more fucked up they became. She would constantly be asking me if I thought Gary's wife was a lesbian, or if any of our friends were gay. Fuck, I loved her, but it drove me crazy, this constant speculation, like all of us were mysteries that we could crack open by the action of our brains. My feeling was that as friends, as family, as members of a neighborhood association, we owed it to the others to take them at their word, their closed blinds, their brusque greetings on the streets. It felt gossipy, particularly with Danny and Marie, because they had been our friends. Our neighbors were all interviewed by the police—this was before my wife had left, you understand—and so whatever speculations they had were encouraged. I know because we were all encouraged to attribute meaning to any tiny transgression or strangeness or outlying car or lurid comment or open window late at night or whatever we had possibly noticed, and in some cases actually logged or blogged or journaled already. These things were wheedled out of us. Anything could matter, they told us. This was important, they told us. Tell us the story. Don't leave anything out.

Here's what I didn't say to them, nor to Katie. I had seen Danny looking at Mary in what I assessed as unfatherly ways more than once. She was fourteen. She was going to be a beauty. She was a beauty already. Which made her a sort of myth. The women were allowed to say it, but the men were not. I don't blame him or think it means any more than it did. And now she was gone. And had any of us entertained our thoughts about what might have transpired? Yes. I'm sure the answer's yes. But, fuck, Danny was already getting the treatment from the police. Everyone assumes the guy's responsible in the absence of another story, another angle to consider the disappearance from and keep it breaking news; of course it would be best if she was found alive, but in the absence of information people are going to talk and fill things in, and it was awful when my wife started doing it. We got into a confrontation over it.

Had I thought about murdering my own wife before? If I'm being honest I'm saying yes. Not to say I would do it, but I had considered it, entertained the thought, let it through the logic gate in my mind and back out into the submerged whatever of it. Had I thought about making out with, off with Mary? That answer is yes also. We can hold a lot of ideas. We can hold a lot of grief. We can wonder if our lives might contain that other thing, just for a moment. Thought is the wrong word. Thought implies intention, which it should not. You are aware of the temptation, what is within you and might erupt at any moment, what you are capable of in spite of all the social interactions and the neighborhood associations: you could tear down anything in your sight. And then you back away from that precipice. You don't have to verbalize it, make it part of a conversation, make it part of the theories on the whiteboard in the police station. You can keep it to yourself, fortress yourself in on weekends, maybe watch a couple of Emmanuelle DVDs and think of the dead. Adjust the sensors on your security system and reconfigure the programmable thermostat. There is a lot to keep you—me, any of us—busy with the world so we don't have to open up our silences.

When Marie died, then, almost two years later to the day, the vans reappeared along the curbs with their transmitting equipment. This time it wasn't the real reporters but the interns or the fact finders or something who were going, again, door-to-door, trying not to appear intrusive, but looking for material. They are always looking for material. Katie asked, Well, could you blame them? They want to know. We all want to know. Do we want to know? I said. Yes we want to know, she said. And pretty soon after that she was gone.

I didn't change much in Katie's office, leaving the things as she had last arranged them. In a way it was just like what Danny did for his daughter. They could both come back. They could both reintegrate themselves into our lives. He had a garage sale after Marie's death, after his family had come in to help him clear out some things and get some distance from it. The whole neighborhood was there at the sale, and lots of random people, maybe looking for items that had some connection to Mary. I bought two alarm clocks, overpaying for them, frankly, at ten bucks a shot, but it felt like doing something. They were nearly identical, still in the package, different colors. His and hers, it read, in a faux-elegant script. I keep them on my nightstand now at home. *Why* is a fine question. Who needs two alarm clocks, and who would put them on the same nightstand? I wish I could say I knew: I think I just wanted to contribute to his forgetting, and seeing them and remembering him helps that, maybe. Most of the stuff he sold was pretty crappy and nondescript. If I were him I'd sell everything I could so that the spaces in his house didn't remind him of Marie. Some of us bought things to remind ourselves of Marie, and some of us of Mary.

Later, I received a note in the mail informing me that I could go down to the station to receive my copy of the police report featuring my shooting and my no more weeping. I had taken to waiting for the mail with suspicion, as if the mailman knew things he wasn't telling about me, about

Katie, about Danny and Marie and Mary, about the final destinations of all of us and our newly separated lives or what remained of them. He had seen the forwarding information, surely, and noticed the decreasing supply of women's magazines to the house. I could see it in his posture as he slid the mail truck up to the driveway, killed the engine, and slumped out toward the door, avoiding eye contact. They must teach you that, I thought, in the training, not to personalize, to avoid confrontation, to carry pepper spray or mace or a Taser in case of dog or other attack. He had to deliver the note from the police in person since it was sent certified mail. He looked at me as I signed it. I said hey, thanks, I appreciate your service. He asked me how I was doing. I said good, good. The weather was looking up again. I asked him if the police ever talked to him about that girl's disappearance, if he had seen anything, if he'd care to add a story to the world. I said I couldn't stop thinking about it. I asked: Could you? But before he could answer, I thought to myself that this was a successful social interaction, so I said never mind and thanks again and have a good one, and I closed the door before he was gone, along with whatever darkness he carried with him on his route, and he started up the truck again and pulled away.

My copy of the police report listed the facts as I described them, which was reassuring. It described the intruder as the decedent, the incident as self-defense, me as shooken up, which I'm fairly sure is not a word. It listed the decedent's name as Lewis Klatt. There were several sections redacted for some reason, blacked out with rough strokes of marker, and the whole thing had been photocopied a couple of times so had that deteriorating look. It didn't contain much information about the decedent. It said his age was seventeen. It did not list his address or surviving relatives.

It took a couple of days before I found his address on the internet. I found his social network page, which had a bunch of sad comments left after his death from those who were his friends. There was no note indicating that the page would be deleted. Oddly he—his mother, probably, learning things she didn't know about her son only after he had left the world—liked a post the day after I shot him. I found his address where he lived with his mother, apparently, his father not being mentioned anywhere. A couple of days later I drove by his place in the evening. It was a four-square, maybe 1,500 square feet, in what Realtors would describe as an emerging neighborhood. A good investment, surely. No lights were on. I wasn't sure what I was doing there as I sat in the heated car. The air was clear. Little was happening on this block. There were no streetlights. The whole place reeked of sadness.

There aren't any streetlights in this city because it is a darkened city with regulations against streetlights on most blocks and the use of halogen headlights, and even powerful flashlights, are discouraged. This is all so as not to interfere with the important work being done at the observatory just past the valley. The trade-off is that we pay more for our police department in the neighborhood where I live, because the lack of light demands more frequent patrols. I parked outside the house. I sat and watched. Nothing happened by virtue of my being there. I wrote a couple of memos to myself and went back home. I could feel something building inside me.

I did not think I wanted forgiveness for shooting the intruder. The report spelled out the justifiability of the situation. I knew I had acted in self-defense, even if I might have been, in retrospect, projecting some of my substantial reservoir of rage about Katie onto the kid and when I shot him he was shot, and Katie was not, and the world waiting outside of teenage girls' windows was not shot or even deterred from whatever they might continue to go on doing, and that was the end of it. And I didn't want any kind of retribution. Or even an encounter with his family. I wanted to rifle through his things. I wanted to break in and achieve the kind of intimacy a person can only gain by breaking into a house. When I broke in, I wanted to find his life laid out for me. What fucked-up things he masturbated to. What things he did beyond his life as described on the social networking page, and we all know you can't trust those facades anyhow.

So I found myself outside the house wearing dark-green-and-black sweatpants. I moved from window to window, sliding out of the security light in front toward the back where nothing was activated by motion. I pressed my hands to each window. There were no pets. In the house there was only silence.

In the back window I could see the flickering LED on what appeared to be an answering machine. It flashed a number, twenty-eight, and had several blinking lights. I tried the latch on the window. It was open. These people, who were these people, who thought nothing of the possibility that someone could come in and take their lives apart?

I entered the window. I waited for something to happen.

I felt like all my life I was waiting for something to happen.

And things did happen to those around me. Katie left or was forced to leave, depending on whom you talked to about it. Danny's life fell apart, his wife, his daughter gone.

And now I was in the decedent's house, leaving a card for the home security company that I used on the kitchen table. Let this be a lesson to you, I thought. Let me make my point this way.

I heard a string of firecrackers going off, maybe a block away. It started my heart up. I thought it was a gun, an uzi maybe, that was how uncomfortable I was in the neighborhood. But that thought receded with the sound into the silence.

I went upstairs. The stairs each creaked distinctively. Though I knew no one was home you never really knew anything about anyone, I thought to myself. What if Danny did it, I thought to myself.

The door read LEWIS: ALL OTHERS STAY OUT, like a kid's. I checked out the other rooms first. Then I opened up his door.

All of his possessions made up a pile on the floor of his room. It looked like it had been searched. The blinds were open and I looked out into the street. Cars passed. I held my breath then let it out. I sat down on the decedent's bed.

The question I had was whether I'd done something unforgivable, or if Katie had, or if anyone had. When I went to college and applied for the requisite set of credit cards, I found out that my parents had been applying for credit in my name for a couple years, having exhausted their own creditworthiness, and my whole score was shot. I was angry. This was years before I met Katie, but the credit traces shadow you for a decade, so I had to explain it to her. She believed me at the time, but later, after she left, she told me she had come to doubt me. I had not forgiven my parents for this, nor for their many other transgressions, and I had told them this, and when they died it didn't change a thing.

Later, when having breakfast with my sister on one of her rare returns to this town, this country, we were talking about this, and she told me she had forgiven me for that time when I had hit her in the head repeatedly with a set of igneous rocks that I had stolen from the church when they had their rock and gem show for kids. She was a little drunk on the mimosas when she told me this. I had not remembered what I was thinking. She said she knew that, that she wondered what I had meant by it. She dabbed off the makeup to show me the scars across the side of her face. I told her I didn't remember that at all. Did I do that? I touched her face. It smelled like lamb. She said there were many things that I had done. Was it possible that she had made up this story for her advantage in future family gatherings? Or were they actual wounds inflicted by my hands? She was twelve, she said. Don't you remember when we had to go to church and when we spent most of our time breaking into the world of Boy Scout paraphernalia hidden away in one of the storage rooms? she said. You know, when you had touched my face and we would listen to muffled hymns being sung a room or two away? I had only vague impressions. I guess it didn't mean that much to me, I said.

The question was whether I had done something unforgivable to Katie, to break her heart and send her away from me, to her many adulteries. Were they a punishment for something I had done? I asked. She said that was stupid, that her affairs were stupid and didn't mean anything, and she was sorry. What did she mean she was sorry? I remember asking. What could anybody mean by that? She had done things. She had done a lot of things. She was not asking for forgiveness, she said. She just felt bad about it and wanted me to know it. I was very angry as I sat on Lewis's cream-colored sheets contemplating his mass of stuff piled on the floor. What a useless set of possessions. It looked like mostly underwear, a couple dozen books, some video game paraphernalia, and, most impressively, a collection of maybe two or three hundred model rocket ships organized in boxes as the base of the heap, all the disposable engines lined up in a long line on the floor. Was that it? I wondered. Was that all he had amounted to?

I had said some things to Katie. I had told her stories about what I might have said or done to Mary in her last moments. Tell that to your gossip columnists, I said. Tell that to the CNN reporters. Are you happy, having wrung that out of me? Her face could not have been whiter. All my blood had drained, too, as this story came out of me. For the first time I can remember she looked utterly surprised. We had crossed a line. I had carried her over the transom into another house, her in another wedding dress and me already naked. And we were held aloft in that moment, suspended somewhere above our marriage and the neighborhood and the rules that the world had set out for us, that we had agreed to. And that lasted for about a minute. And then her expression turned, and she had turned, and she had gone, and that was it, and was it possible that that was really it at last? I had been drunk just as I was drunk with my sister, receiving her drunken forgiveness as she sobbed. They both were sobbing. I was not sobbing. I didn't sob when I shot the intruder down. I did not believe in this catharsis. I would finger all my wounds and allow that pain to penetrate. I would bathe in it, fortify myself with it.

I paused. I kept waiting for something to happen.

If this scene turned out as I hoped, I would hear the shrieks of the stairs, the clicks of weapons being armed. The door would open suddenly and the room would fill with the sound of angry voices. I would feel nothing as I lay back on the decedent's bed, pants around my ankles, headphones on, as I pleased myself furiously, thinking of all of you, your naked bodies, your open mouths. I would barely be aware of any force as gunshots bloomed across my chest like a spring field on fast-forward. Time would slow and somebody would understand something, and I would at last be carried away by consequence.

Believing in the Future with the Torturer's Apprentice

I left but then returned in the after of after, when the world was mostly smoke and the air was completely ruined, without telling my husband or his other wife, those other girls with his eyes and her hair that I found under the stairs. We had agreed to leave it all behind. The silver vessels. The 132 Couroc trays I had collected. Our wedding rings. The cat's ashes. My mother's. The stinky sinks that you could never fully clean, not with help, not ever. The hair clustered in the drains. The geologic rings of calcium around the pool. The still-boxed Christmas lights. The speculum. The college syllabi. Love letters. Computers. The photographs of pain that were his life's work, women's mouths, mostly, frozen, opening into the acrid air. They were saying untold things, only my husband knows just what, and now they weren't saying anything. They were burning. They had probably already burned.

It took almost a decade to feel that I could believe in him fully. He did, after all, have another spouse. Another house. Two kids in the photographs he hid away from me in the cubby below the stairs. We had none. He hadn't wanted another one. It didn't bother me. I said it didn't bother me. It was easier this way. I had my portion of the space. I didn't need him every day. I got my way enough. I had my work enough, my friends enough. I was coughing less and less, the lifetime of whatever it was in my lungs finally clearing up.

The press called him "the torturer's apprentice." The phrase was apt, though he disliked it. You know his mentor better: the more famous artist, the one who goes without a name. He used just a pompous little glyph. Which drove people crazy. But my husband, the lesser known, he has a name. He's the one who's into mouths. He prepared the girls. He did the contracts up. The glyph wouldn't do the contracts or the casting. Like a wizard, he wouldn't appear until the girls were prepped and ready, until they'd been emptied out. All the materials had to be there before he showed. And he wouldn't stay after. My husband the apprentice took his photos while they were still in prep. Then the glyph did his famous thing. Then the girls went home. Sometimes they came to the gallery shows, signed autographs, editions. When they did they seemed oddly blank. They said they didn't remember anything. They looked like they were haloed in light, like they were levitating.

My husband showed me the studio. An operating room, totally clean and bare and chemical and steel. Restraints. One-way mirrors. It's fucked up. I'm the first one to tell you it's fucked up. I've always known it is. But it is honest. Deep down all of us are fucked. It takes a special something to bring that out so far, so fast from us. The two of them may be reviled, but no one looks away. In our world no one ever looks away.

The secret with my husband's photographs is that you can't fully tell what they're about, orgasm or agony, groan or moan or first speech or hum, if there is a difference, either way it's something emerging, not yet fully formed, a breath between breaths, an aperture opening, and a way to punctuate a day, a night, a life. The close-up of the mouth is where it's at for him. The folded vee of tongue. The lemniscate of lips closed then opening. A mouth is like a flower, he said. A mouth is like a bird. A mouth is like a tease. A feet with toes unfurling. A mouth is like a fountain.

I said, no, a mouth is like a hive of bees, slow cave-in, being hanged, a bomb.

You can't deny it moves you, he said. You can tell it does something to you.

The time elapsed between the photographs is short. The time between his publication of the photographs and the girls' release was short. Their skirts were short. It was always skirts. It was always girls. This world. It's a little sick. That's what makes it good, he said. They signed up for it. They confessed. They opened up. They released their secrets and were released. That's the trick to it, that it's not just release of voice, it's not fake or forced. It was their choice. Everyone has them, choices, secrets, voice boxes, constraints, restraints. If pressed hard enough we will all become swans.

The torture is not the point. The point is the joint between the time before and the time after. The crux. That photograph—not representing time, but time itself. That crossing space. This used to be the world. Now this is the world. Sometimes, the worlds, they seem the same. You can barely tell the difference. Clouds before. Clouds here after. But something's changed. You can feel it. If you look close enough, the seam. The way we work out memories, what gets stored, starred for later easy retrieval, what gets discarded, boarded up. How a moment—an accident, a gas explosion, a runaway train, spreading sudden fire, a dozing driver on the interstate, fragment of falling satellite, an affair, a series of affairs, hair loss, a decapitation from a sheet of glass like in *The Omen*, power surge at the wrong time, power line drooping in the pool, anaphylactic shock, lightning strike, band saw slip, not to mention rapture, heart attack, stroke, or other ways the body can up and fail us—these are abysses with no bottom. Narrative works like this. Our lives work like this. Our lives are not narrative except as synapse makes them so.

If he needed to photograph it, which he did, needing to document it—I accepted that. He had nodded off in an ether haze in the medieval-themed Best Western (formerly the Sybaris, where we used to meet in the early days of our affair: now it's under new management, but it still takes cash and asks no questions), so I clicked on his camera. There were sixty-six shots of the fireball going up, our house bursting with gas, our stuff being converted to flame, and one close-up of a mouth. My mouth. Was I laughing? I wasn't sure.

He didn't need to know I would go back. We agreed there would be no going back. It made sense. We left the cars; otherwise they would know. Ditto with the clothes, the photographs. The pornographic DVDs that we hadn't watched for years. The two irreplaceable pieces of his mentor's work. Anything that meant anything had to stay, to burn. Needless to say there could be no note or explanation.

Since he didn't need to know, I took the rental car back. It was dark, but I knew the route. I wore a wig. I wore a skirt. In my old life I never wore a skirt. Was I an object or a subject in the skirt? As I watched from down the block, I could see my mouth, an apparition in the daylight side of the rearview, and, surprised, I closed it. I disappeared.

Ours was not the first to burn. For the last week, town houses in the hills around had been going up like far-off Christmas lights. It was festive. I'd have a drink each time. Plumes of gas erupted through roofs, followed by the slow wind of sirens up the curling streets. I couldn't sleep so I would watch them go. Sometimes I would take the car to get a closer look. Faulty gaslines were blamed. Weak hearts were blamed.

Electrical fires were blamed. Houses not up to code. Arson, maybe, the police started to think. Just bad luck, said others. A psychic said consult your ghosts, but no one knew what to do with that. The more houses that disappeared the more I started to think about disappearing myself. I didn't know where that feeling came from, but what I knew is that I wanted me gone, us gone, the whole record of us and who we had decided to be gone. We, too, could be swans, I said. We could come out of this something else.

It was a calculated risk. It's not as if I wasn't willing to share him. To be sure, I didn't want him more than occasionally. His other wife, that family, I knew almost nothing about. He wanted it that way. I didn't even know their names. I didn't want to know their names. He said that way it would be pure. Prudent. Unputrefiable. He knew how women were, he said. He knew how knowing could weigh you down.

It took him ten years to give up his secrets, for us to have a future we could finally believe in together, for us to have no space between us, for us to have all-access passes. That's why he loves me now, because I can know and hold his secrets suspended in my body and not hate him for them. Because I understood. Because I said I understood. When I knew them all, that knowing was really something. That's why I really stayed, that sense of ownership, of openness: we were a pane of glass. I couldn't stand the opaque house, his second house, the constant smell of gas, the unbroken winter sunlight, the flimsy walls that could barely keep the howls of the neighbors' dogs outside, our sex lives in. The whole neighborhood, Lakewood Grove, had no lakes, no wood, no groves. The whole place was a fiction, a city without city things like a government or police force. It had no past. We had no past. We were pressed flat. We were drying paper. Without a past what were we? A moment in a photograph?

I didn't miss the house then and I don't miss it now. Now the house is gone and so are we, except in memory. We're someone else, I think.

Even so when I went back without his knowledge I took just one thing: a picture of the ash.

What else he doesn't know is this: I take my own photographs when he's asleep. I pet his throat. Subtly pluck his eyebrows. I tease his lips apart. I pry his eyelids slowly open like a clam. I touch the eye. Roll it in its orbit. Sometimes I spit on it. Interrogate it. Put small objects in the mouth. Make him swallow and wonder later. He can't tell. He'll never tell or know. He takes these sleeping pills because of restlessness.

I can do whatever to his mouth when he is out. The drugs make him suggestible. This is my mouth, I whisper, breathing onion on him. I exfoliate his skin. Peel his lips. Watch his muscles move involuntarily. Stroke his teeth. Depress the tongue. This has been going on a year. When will it be enough? I wonder. It's not art, I said. It's something else.

The Golem

And now the fallen monster was apparent, Annette thought, as Terence let himself out and her husband emerged from the kitchen, where he had been the whole time. It was him. Or maybe it was her. Or maybe Terence. Someone here was clearly the monster.

Harry was writing about it already. She could hear the keys clicking.

As she dressed again the cat clambered up into her lap with force. It started to knead her and purr. Whose dream was this? she wondered as it stared at her possessively, its eyes half-moons, inches from her face. It hurt, she admitted, as its claws worried through the fabric, but it was warm. It was possibly thinking about eating her whole. She hadn't considered this before.

So this nightmare had been released and was out in the world. And had she enjoyed it? If so, it would serve him right, wouldn't it? As it had been his idea. He had hoped to—what? Get some ideas for his half-birthed novel? Develop his sense of loathing further? Fine-tune his own self-laceration? The cat's breath was in her face: not as bad as she'd thought, she guessed. She didn't know what to say about it now. At least there hadn't been a camera.

Harry had asked for that but she had had the sense to say no to that one request, she thought. She congratulated herself. But wouldn't it be just as bad to have the incident recorded in his fiction, where maybe no one else would know it but she would know it, senseless and needy, hydroencephalytic. It, now IT, would sit there in all caps, dramatic, an IT generated by whatever electricity was left between the two of them and become something new: the word made flesh made word. And it would move, slowly at first. Perhaps it would start to strut. If Harry did it right, soon it would begin to sing.

The cat continued its methodology around her chest. The beast was driven by something deeper, but what that was she couldn't say.

The cat had come to her, not him. That would begin to mean something later, she thought. Maybe it was a symbol. Maybe she would start writing something in response.

It wasn't even the middle of the night, and already he was straying, her husband, who would worry at this like a scar. Annette had been the good wife, willing, or was that it? She couldn't see herself that easily, not like usual, not right now. She had played this role. He had asked and she had said yes, meaning something else then, but what had it become?

"It meant nothing," she would tell him later. That would slip out.

"Of course it did," he said. "It was nothing. How could it mean anything?"

"Was it good for you," she asked, suddenly cruel. "Was it for you, or was it for me?" She'd bored quickly, and now thought this conversation stupid.

"You really don't know?" Harry asked, and then he didn't either, the more he thought about it. It was his dream made real, he supposed. He had read about it years before, or maybe thought it up out of nothing. Or had it come from a scene he barely could remember from pornography stashed away in the closet in the house, one of his father's many treasures. And what did it matter where it came from, since it had now arrived. The pages of the magazines were glossy and they smelled of something. Whiskey, maybe. Cologne, probably. Neglect. He had quite a collection. Harry couldn't remember the words at all, but the images, they were pressed into him: legs, spread; eyes, were they looking at him? What did she imagine was in him then? The toenail curl. And it was powerful. Harry could see that much, what it did to her. What it did to him. Things were changing fast. The cat was on her lap, having settled in. He could see its shadow on her face by the angle of the light. It was, would be, a weight between them for years. Or at any rate, he thought, this was something they could share, which was true.

The cat could barely move. Someone had to take it in after his father died, and certainly not his brother, who was overseas and anyway would never, not even punctuating his absence with the comma of a visit for the funeral. Matters were decided by TELEX, a dying service that had the benefit of being fully legal in the eyes of the law. Like his marriage, he supposed, ha ha. And what it was or could be, what it could be remade to be in this story he was working on. It would be ugly: a new effect for him.

Could he look at her again, he wondered, without seeing Terence, who was even now an afterthought, a poltergeist, whatever kind of image is left behind after staring at something for a year compressed into an hour, like a ringing in the retina's memory, and he hadn't even seen it firsthand, couldn't bring himself to do that exactly, to watch the two of them go at it like animals. That's what they were. He had heard enough. So he had taped it, even as he had promised her on his father's memory not to do. He wanted it mediated through the camera, as if that could burn him less.

He would watch the whole thing later if he could bear it, if he could ever bear it, which he expected he could not, but he couldn't bear not knowing either. He watched the cat's weight press down on Annette. It would serve her right. That pleasure would serve her right. He wasn't sure, he thought—just maybe—it was just a germ of a thought, really, not even developed, but there, a seed in the heart, something around which the two of them could grow—he thought it a necessary wound, like it might open her. Maybe it was something bigger, though, a shadow cast by the chair, woman, and cat combined. Now he wanted to stomp its stupid heart out. And the two of them just sitting there, all linoleum and redirected light.

The feeling spread, reaching everywhere. Growing, kowtowing to nothing, maybe, like that cat, which had gotten even bigger after his dad had finally died, like it absorbed some part of him, if it was possible, if his dad's death had even happened. The more he thought about it the less he could recall. He could see scenes recorded in his memory, but what good was that if you didn't have it on tape or etched on paper somewhere?

He had agreed to take the cat, but now it might as well have always been Annette's.

And besides, did she get off or was she playing? It sounded like it did, and suddenly he was ashamed, sort of.

That feeling could power a plot: of that he was sure. He could feel its wringing in him even now, even if he didn't know how to hold or shape it yet. Who knew how big it could get if he let it grow?

There was a light suddenly on outside and Annette closed her eyes. Motion detector probably. She could hear a shriek, maybe human, maybe not.

The cat jumped off her suddenly and silently, no claws, the movement surprising them both. Nothing was light out there except the occasional passing car. Would it be better if it was daytime and they could both see the world for what it was? she thought. It was a wreck, but harmless. Everything was there right in front of them, suspended in the air between them like in one of many strong magnetic fields. Annette felt sick, and wondered if this was the beginning of a child inside her or just another stupid feeling. It was possible—you had to admit that it was in spite of everything—and what would that mean? The word made flesh made flesh forever, a harder memory to erase.

Harry stood and left the room like he was the wounded one. He would sulk, maybe, go interior; he would leave her alone. The owl pictures on the walls leered at her and his retreating back. They had nothing good to say.

She wouldn't tell him yet of this spark of sickness unless she needed to deploy it. It could be her body in revolt. It could be her anger, or a curl of the cancer in her, suddenly reawakened. Wouldn't that teach him something, she thought, and regretted it immediately. He could lie in his bed thinking of it. The adolescent thought: maybe it could be something to remember her by when she was gone, that story unreeling in his mind. She could feel an action in her body. Did he watch, she thought: that was the question. He must have wanted to, to see what it could be like. How much of that could he take? Annette asked herself. Would Harry be the kind who wouldn't watch, who would take some solace in that dignity, or the kind who would bludgeon her with his virtue? He was awfully visual. She knew all about what flashed on his screens after she had gone to sleep—and knowing, she could feel herself getting in a rut, and what did that say about her marriage, if that's what you could call it, now.

But she had done what he had asked, and maybe she had wanted it too. Obviously some part of her had relished the act or its effect. It was a kind of ugly satisfaction, like Terence's scarred thumb stumps: Was it a fetish feeling she was having? Was it at Terence's expense? It did contain him a little when she thought it, and she liked the way it felt, so she continued.

He had lost them years before in an accident with a printing press, he had said, and after, his scarred body being the first thing others would notice, he focused entirely on his body, covering himself with tattoos of hands and stars and hands on stars and stars on hands. It was something to see, she had to admit. It had power, which was part of why she'd consented—eventually. Terence had become all flesh, trim, a stock car—muscle, torque, and movement—nothing like a Harry, maybe, if you even had to make that comparison, which she never admitted to, or if she did, she wouldn't tell him. She turned her head. She could still see him and the marks he'd made all along his body. She could still feel the way he felt above her.

From his office Harry could see the grill on the patio below, hunched under its expensive cover, and beyond the trees there was the arroyo, and he couldn't see past that. The grill cast a little shadow from the security light that flicked on when something passed through its field of vision. It was usually an animal, he presumed, but often he was too slow to see what had triggered it.

Harry's hands were in motion on the keyboard, trying to make himself a memory, trying to metabolize it or pass it through him like a stone. It was his father's grill: another artifact of his passing. It was shiny chrome, or steel probably, one of those distinctions that had never come easily for him, and it was charcoal with a gas starter, and if left uncovered it seemed to glow, even at night. The effect was creepy, almost unearthly, and had unsettled him enough that he'd bought a custom cover to stop its shining. The grill was no longer in production, and a generic cover (he'd tried a few) just blew off when the wind came up. He wondered if his father had ever contemplated this same light at night, maybe looking down from a window like this one in the old house, and if he did, what he'd made of the effect. Harry had never known to ask until it was no longer possible to, and now he couldn't shake the question. Was it a talisman, a portent, or just how light worked in the dark? He wondered about this, to no end, at night, in circles, until he took the pill that shut it down. This was perhaps his problem, this tendency for overanalysis, possibly also inherited or learned, this worrying over the problem with his hands, with his mind. It did no one any good, but that didn't change anything at all, he knew.

What made this night's event special was that they had actually made something new, even if none of them could know it now. What were their obligations to Terence, and what should he know later, and when?

Terence was obviously just a guy, an interloper who had agreed to play this role. And it hadn't taken much, had it? He could see that even when he agreed, and what did this say about him? He had guaranteed that he was clean, which he was not, but that's what you get from a situation like this, Terence told himself later. He had left as quickly as he could because something was clearly happening between the two of them. Annette he would remember, of course, as he did most of his conquests, if it was fair to call her that. Maybe he was the conquest, he thought immediately but let it drop, and even so, even with her husband in the other room, okay with it, or even spitefully okay with it, trying to prove something to the two of them, or to the three of them: even then he counted it as his. He didn't notch his bedpost, though he did take a kind of pride in the performance, though that wouldn't last, it never did, and he would be returned to what he was before. Still you took your pleasure where you could get it, and so Terence left them to the remainder, the whatever that it was: he could feel himself growing in the room, his body cool, fresh with disappearing sweat, becoming monstrous the more he waited, until he couldn't bear it, and he left.

Harry and Annette were not the first he had played this role for. It was a niche, he guessed. It seemed more and more likely that it was, as it happened again and again, and what should he take away from that, from this fact that people could just read it in him—maybe it was a mark he bore or in his countenance?

His specialty was accepting propositions. He would be the wedge the couple would drive into itself. He was literally the wedge. He would open them up, those couples, those legs, sometimes both sets of them in the same bed, or in dreams after, and he would be happy with it, or if not happy, then it wouldn't bother him. He had sometimes been recorded, and existed now on tape or in tens of thousands of scattered bits across hard drives, people wanting something to watch for a while, an actor standing in for them or for whatever was between them, could come between them: he didn't care what they'd made, and didn't care why he was chosen, why he played this role and not others. He was filled with light, he felt. Made of it increasingly. He drew it from the world when he went out in daytime, and gave it off in the later portion of the nights when they'd done something like this. Maybe he'd even be famous if they released the tapes on the net as someone would surely eventually do, and he would be admired years from now for the quality of his thrusting or something similar, the marks all along his body, his particular com-

memoration of his old pain, the dimples in his cheeks, some outstand-
ing, shining trait, and he would be embraced in this way, too, and maybe
even redeemed for the things that he had—that we all had—done.

What they had made was not a baby exactly.

Would it surprise them to know that it had risen, or perhaps been
summoned, in their triangle of electric pull and disregard? It came to life
down in the arroyo where the trash collected when it rained. At first the
size of a comma on a page in an instruction manual for home wiring
projects, it bent a little, then it bulged, and then it grew and split: a semi-
colon, then a letter, an en dash, and then an em, and then a word, and
then it stretched into a sentence.

Nothing registered its first movements. It wouldn't have seemed like
much by then anyhow: a string of sentences glued or hinged together.
You know how a stick bug only looks like a stick if you see it on a stick,
and otherwise it looks like nothing? This too. It looked like something
you'd want to stomp, and maybe you should if you'd noticed it. All there
was down in the arroyo were teenagers anyhow, engaged in pursuit of
sex or violence or fuckoffery, some dissenting or just drug-fueled adven-
ture out of sight of their parents and their friends. By definition, what
happened down here in the runoff didn't matter, they figured, and whatever they were interested in, it was the opposite of books. Break, fuck,
or fuck with what you want. Burn the rest. There was nothing to believe
in except for trash and fire. The rest of us rightly didn't think about it
that much.

An hour later, unnoticed and unstomped, the thing took its first step
off the page. It simply lifted itself up perpendicular to the page's surface
and left it behind. Now it was out and in the air.

From there it climbed over a *Paul Blart: Mall Cop 2* DVD and peered
over the junk pile toward the electric towers through which ran the lines
that connected the development to others.

Peered may not be the word. It surely wondered—and likely compre-
hended—nothing. It thought nothing. But it did seem as if it took stock
of its new dimensionality, and it did seem to be looking for something.
Then it began to walk—really, it shuffle-dragged—in a direct line to Harry
and Annette's house.

It was still dark. They had by now settled into a detente, each of them
grooming their own hurts and thinking about what the other would have
to say to be forgiven.

Terence nurtured his story, too, in another house, surrounded by his memories of the event: how it felt, not what it meant. He masturbated to stop the feeling of thinking about it. If he understood more about what had happened, he didn't say. He'd seen some shit, of course. He knew what went on in homes.

He didn't call, and didn't expect a call. He kept his phone on just in case.

Hours passed in this way. Each of them slept some.

The thing approached Harry and Annette's house. It had grown again. Thigh-high now, it had been partly torn in a bother with a dog, so it dragged a dangling clause behind it like a chain. It circled the house, pressed its face and hands to the bay window in the living room. It began to spread. Beginning there, it papered over each window and door while they slept.

When Harry and Annette awoke in separate beds and saw no light, they still thought it night. In the room they had once hoped to make a nursery, Harry cracked an eye, seeking a little moonlight reassurance. Finding none, he closed his eyes again. Annette, restless in the bedroom, stretched out an arm toward the side where her husband usually slept. Of course the cat was in his space. She ran her fingers through its fur. She could feel it look at her. It would always look at her.

None of them would ever leave the house again.

When it had completed its bloody work, Harry and Annette and the history of their marriage and all their angers and ambitions, all their thrills and spells, had been reduced and bound to a series of sentences on a page.

When you have finished reading it they will be gone.

The Reassurances

Sharon had said that it was real goddamn romantic that I'd finally done it, proposed like that, with an adopt-a-road sign with her name writ large, though I couldn't quite tell if she meant it. I felt I'd chosen a perfect piece of interstate, a long upslope where everyone trailed out of the city on the hottest days toward the cooler mountain promise and had plenty of time to read as they climbed, hoping not to stall. Inevitably cars overheated and pulled off to the side, and the rest of the traffic slowed to take in their failure, and in that moment, I thought, Sharon's name and my proposal would be there to say oh yea, verily, there is still love in this overheating world.

You could choose up to ten miles of road, but I picked only four: it seemed enough to be a major undertaking yet not ostentatious enough to dominate the commute to her parents' cabin on the lake that was once a meteor strike some hundred thousand years before, they'd said, and was now a perfect crater finned most days by Jet Skis and pontoon boats and people pissing into the water and the rest of the people trying to ignore the fact of the increasingly piss-filled water. Well, she said, it's all piss-filled, isn't it? The job of living is not to think about it too much, since it'll paralyze you. True, I thought, I was easily paralyzed by exactly this kind of consideration. I thought but didn't say this is why I need you.

On hot days, which came more and more frequently it felt like, the whole world heating and shifting climate toward the North, the exodus from the city might look from above like bacterial colonies, thousands of them in clumps and globs and slow-motion lines, coalescing and breaking apart and moving away from the equator. I'd never seen it that way but I could imagine.

That she would not say yes I had not counted on, nor that she would shortly thereafter be killed in a car accident, an irony that did not escape me in my self-serving grief (it increasingly approached woe, it seemed), nor that she would—within an hour of her death, or what the outside world understood as death, and scientifically the line between the two, alive and dead, was never quite as firm as we believed—be transferred to frozen storage in Phoenix that her parents had purchased for her instead of a car when she'd turned sixteen. I had not foreseen that she would be cryonically frozen before what was left of her skin had given away its warmth, that she would then be preserved in perpetuity, catastrophically contused but unfortunately not entirely gone.

All this was terrible of course, and it was worse for her to be so near—twenty-two miles away by cloverleaf and car and merge and merge and merge—but so far, kept from me by a wheel of glass and steel and frost and the supercooled liquid she was now suspended in. The preservation cocktail they used changed constantly, their scientists reported, as they conducted new research and improved their modeling, and got access to nanomaterials and therapies until then legal only in shady countries. I only got to see her once, and only by proxy, in a video taken by her mother, shown at the strange sort-of wake they'd held (they called it The Believing), and watching it was weird and hard enough to make me unsure I'd ever want to see her again or that in fact I even could. She was close, but off limits since I had not yet been put on the visiting list, and besides, driving in the city has been getting harder on account of the bombings.

They weren't big bombs, the television said, but they were enough to bring down a structural support of a bit of interstate. The explosions did not strike terror in my heart, but they did add another thirty minutes to the drive, giving me one more reason not to go see my not-quite-dead former almost fiancée in not-quite-person.

Terry and Charles—Charles, her mother, a dominant woman with a man's name, which led to no end of awkwardnesses at introductions to boyfriends, past and present, I was sure—explained it to me straight: it was her belief, they said, that the conditions that would presently lead to death might in fact be remedied in the future, not too far off even. I'd never heard Sharon talk about that, or death at all except in the abstract or in the distant past. Only forty years ago, for instance, Charles explained, we were still performing lobotomies, doing electroshock. A hundred years ago we had no cure for polio. Did you know, she said, that scientists were at this very moment supercooling patients in liquid daily to slow down aging? That they've successfully frozen organs in

order to transport them for transplant? That the average American
wood frog freezes solid multiple times every winter and lives to hop
again in spring? Their bodies actually turn to a form of glass, she said,
and back to flesh when the cold has passed and spring has sprung. Did
you know that? And glass is not a solid: made from cooling liquid, it's
not completely finished being a liquid and not yet a solid, so it's something in between. I mean, we think we know what death and illness is,
she said: we think we've conquered the body. But so we always had, and
we were wrong then. Why not think we might be wrong now? Why not
take a shot on belief instead? And isn't that what a proposal is? Imagine,
she said, spreading out her hands in a way I assumed she had practiced
many times in private before deploying it in instances like this, what the
future might bring for our dear girl.

I can't, I said.

Exactly my point, she said.

When you put it that way, the prospect did sound compelling.

Her stasis, as they called it, or sometimes cryonic sleep, meant that they
could not close off that part of her that they kept alive. For instance,
her room at home remained the same, even as her body was preserved
in the city. She was their only child, and they had such hopes for her,
Charles explained in tears over an exotic African tea she had bought
online, we could see it coming, her future, her family, her children, the
whole future of their bloodline. Your bloodline, she said. Was it strange
to say it like that, she asked, like she was a commodity? She wasn't and
she was, she said. Wait until you have kids. Then you'll get it. They're
how we leave the world, she said. That's why they hadn't done so much
as put away the mismatched socks she'd left in the shape of a flower on
the bed the last time she'd been home. You never know, they said, if she
came back, what might spark her into who she used to be before. The
steam curlicued from our cups like question marks.

In these conversations I couldn't ever tell where I stood, what they
expected of me. Was I another vector pointing toward my almost fiancée
and the future they imagined, and was I expected to keep pointing in
her direction indefinitely, hoping for a medical miracle? Did they know,
for instance, that she had said no to my engagement overture? We had
kept dating, and I doubted she'd been straight with them. It wasn't one
of those moments where it was marriage now or nothing, she explained,
she'd hoped I'd understand. It wasn't that it wasn't me. And it wasn't that

it was her. She felt safe, she said. She wasn't sure what that meant, she said, not yet.

It hurt a lot to hear. Was it not big enough, the ask? I asked. She said you don't understand, and I didn't, it was true. She said I want you in my life and in my home. She said just give me time. Okay, I said. And we had left it at that. I had no idea how to nudge her needle, and now it was stuck there, in memory, unnudgeable, unneedleable: I couldn't push it in and couldn't pluck it out. What secrets did she take with her? Now I would never know exactly what it was she was waiting for and what I was trying so hard to hold on to.

I want to be honest here: in my darkest moments after she'd pressed pause on our future, I'd had the thought that my love was shallow and foul, and everyone saw me for who and what I was, but somehow I couldn't see it. I didn't tell anyone this because, as my former therapist had explained some years before, I had a habit of making others' pain about myself. It was a childhood thing. It didn't help, he'd said.

It took a year for Terry and Charles to get back to their habit of hosting weekend parties. It was different now without their daughter, who became an unavoidable subtext for all the action that followed. The parties still bumped and sheared and veered off course when it got overlate and people were on their own longer, looking at the stars, which were everywhere up here once you got out of the metro area and the ceiling of fog and smoke, only some of which was the result of the bombings: it was like there wasn't anything obscuring them from you or you from them, and what if we all were high or drunk, barely connecting, if we ever did at all, and before I knew it one of the two—they traded off—would start something and it would lead to, in one case, a grill being kicked over and starting the ramada on fire.

I was there for this event. I watched it. I was drunk, too, I should say, since I didn't see how I could get through the party sober. I don't know what set it off, but it was Charles who started teasing Terry, someone said, she had started it, but he had finished it, kicking it over with the chicken still inside. He was smoking it—it was one of those egg-shaped grills that took forever to cook anything—and I remember turning to watch what seemed like a whole beach of burning coals, like a lava flow I'd seen on TV reaching the sea in some island country, spreading on the concrete slab they'd had inexplicably stained black, and into the garden beyond. It held the heat, the paint-black slab, longer than it should, and now it was covered up with char. I wondered if the plants would light, and I watched anticipating it for a moment, before it was clear nothing was going to happen. And Terry left the coals there on the slab with the half-cooked chicken. Fuck it was all he said. Let it burn itself out. I'm done with this.

I wondered if he'd meant me. I was still invited to the parties, and I was glad for the invitations. Charles had called and left a voicemail saying how much they hoped I would come, but I found Terry's silence even more opaque than Charles's ostentatious attempts at connection. She was always the one who made the calls—to everyone, I supposed. I don't think I'd ever talked to Terry on the phone. It was possible she meant the opposite, that she would have preferred that I let myself out quietly from their lives by the back door, but I didn't think it likely. After all, they'd put me on their cell phone plan; they'd given me Sharon's old phone in spite of how she'd had it laser-etched and bedazzled. You might as well use it, Charles had told me. It made it through the accident, and that must mean something. And in her state she can't, she'd said, and had laughed in that flat way. I could never quite figure out if she'd understood it as a joke or not until she said it, and maybe not even then.

I stood there watching the coals smolder after everyone else had moved back inside, like I'd missed the memo. I told Terry that I'd nurse my beer and keep watch in case something caught on fire. I don't know if he didn't hear me or didn't care, but no one seemed to mind that I didn't rejoin the group in the living room, so instead I turned to look up at Sharon's window and then out over the garden. It was an okay garden, the kind you grew in Arizona, meaning small and weird and weak. A couple of rows of tomato plants on drip irrigation. Everyone loves tomatoes. A rosemary bush was taking over a concrete bench they'd had as long as I'd known them. Some kind of freaky mini-squashes now were covered in the grill sludge. With everything else blanketed in ash, I could see a little red-capped garden gnome I'd never noticed before crossing his arms as if in disapproval. The light and sound of laughing from inside reflected off his face.

I also had not counted on the fact that I was now doomed to five years of collecting trash by hand from my four miles of motorway, those miles that once led to our future lives together and now led to a spectacular sort of disappointment. I spent one day each month walking those same four miles chucking cans and paper lids and piss bottles and unidentifiable fruit and receipts and cigarettes and broken toys and scratched-up mix CDs that were typically unplayable (I did check and try to play them; I treated them as I treated all the trash I found those years: as auguries) and diapers filled with shit and blood and worse and things that were simply beyond identification, that defied human category, and pulled them into bags and leaving them like little lunches on the sides of roads to be picked up by the state. One time I thought I found a couple of thumbs but the police told me they were chicken bones.

It is not wrong to say I did watch the road, as the safety orientation instructed, not only for weaving cars but also for her parents' weaving car. Terry had nearly hit me once, though I don't know that he knew it was me cleaning up this stretch of road with his daughter's name emblazoned all along it. I caught a flash of his face at speed as I had to dive back into the median to avoid him. It was all wet then, a rarity for the desert. It had rained, and the water had pooled everywhere. It was supposed to drain but didn't. I'd cleaned the grates in the median in that section already so was pretty sure nothing truly hazardous was down in there blocking the water. I had to put in a maintenance request to the DOT to check the section for a possible obstruction.

I had chosen the adopt-a-road stratagem because I'd seen my uncle memorialized that way and I know he'd have loved to see the whole family out every couple of months in their orange reflective vests and hats spearing roadside trash like we were prisoners. He'd always known, he'd said, that we were a couple of strokes of bad luck away from a life of crime. He was talking about me then: he still thought he could save me from the way our family went. He was also talking about my brother, who was substantially more successful but possibly even less happy, at least before the car accident that killed my almost fiancée, at which point all the balance sheets of our collective woe shifted to me, and I used it as a reason to stop returning everybody's calls.

You might not know but you can pay to have your section cleaned instead of doing it yourself. If you stop cleaning up your section, though, you can be hit with hefty fines. They can and will put a lien on your property. They take this task seriously, they say. People crap out of it all the time. It's a drain on the state, they said.

I explained the situation to the DOT on the phone: She said no, I said. And what's more, she has since died, I said. And what's worse, I said, is that her body was now preserved down at the cryonics lab, and the worst of all is that I'm not on the list of acceptable visitors, as I've been branded by the family and the lab a disbeliever, no matter how well we get along, and have been informed that my sort of negativity is not conducive to recovery, so I am not allowed beyond the interview rooms upstairs. But the DOT would not relent. They were very sorry for my loss, they said. But a contract is a contract, and what you're doing is important, especially with the traffic getting rerouted in the city on account of recent events. I could, however, subcontract my miles to a company, they said. They gave me some names that I wrote down but then threw out.

For your sign they don't let you use a phrase. It has to be the name of a person, organization, or corporation, like those are the only things that are important. So I did what I had to do to get it on the sign. You can't say I didn't take this all the way. I started up an LLC. I registered its name as Sharon, Marry Me, and the commas are included in the name. It was a fight to get them preserved. It was a brand, I said, and punctuation matters.

I think sometimes how other Sharons in their cars on their way to or from the lakes might still see that proposal, and their hearts might light up, flicker to life, as if they were getting power from a gas generator, just for a moment, thinking, Oh my god, is this me? Even the married ones might pause seeing it, wondering at the gesture I had made, feeling themselves loved again by proxy, seeing that there were still romantic gestures in the world. But how long would that astonishment last? Would that feeling fade as they passed it again and again en route to their city homes or work? And would they wonder at what had happened to it when it had gone, how they had become inured to wonder?

It took a year, but eventually I got a job at the Core Facility, as it was called. My history degree seemed to lend itself to maintenance, I explained in my interview. Because of what I had read and seen of the delusions of the past, I knew how things went wrong, how we always believe we know the world but don't, not really. They'd asked about my feelings on cryonics. I had meant to lie. I had this whole thing planned, but in the moment I said I don't pretend to know. Once I did, and disbelieved, I said, but now I don't, some things happen in your life without a reason, and so who's to judge what someone else believes? Some people hope, I said. Some of us want to believe.

I had originally applied in sales but they sized me up in the first moment of the interview in the gleaming, faceless room, and said listen, we can tell, you're not sales, it's okay, it takes a special kind of personality to do sales; we have another job for you. All I had to do, I knew, was say that I believed, or could, or wanted to. This company was a pyramid built on belief. It was also an actual pyramid, the offices, tinted glass and steel, an accomplishment of branding, though before it was a cryonics lab it was a bank that failed. I don't know how they found it, but the first thing you thought when you saw it was pharaohs, and look how long they lasted and how much we know about their afterlives.

Anyhow, they were right about sales not being right for me, and they made me an offer and I took it. It paid well, better than what I had made before, which allowed me to start to take a bite out of all those student loans. And one benefit of working there, they explained, was that I got a break on their services. I was obliged, in fact, to sign up for the minimum plan. It was because they needed to say, they explained, that all of their employees weren't just employees; they were also clients, all the way down, even way down in maintenance.

Well, I didn't believe, but what was there to lose, I figured. The minimum plan called for preservation of the head and head alone, and was good for twenty years, at which point you or your estate would have to pay a yearly fee to avoid decrepitude or disposal, which felt only a little like a threat.

It remains unclear who is perpetrating the bombings. At first the police weren't sure they were even bombings. Since the real estate crash whole swaths of the Phoenix sprawl aren't populated or surveilled. Companies build and fail and move to the next thing to build. So when the first bombs took down unleased office buildings in empty office parks, they were not exactly missed. People figured it was probably a new development they were putting in, and maybe some paperwork had been missed, but when the ruins stayed ruined for a month after that and a fire started burning in the rubble and the sirens came in to put it out, only then did anyone even check, and then arson got mentioned. An insurance fire, probably. When that got reported on the news, people started writing in to the television stations to claim responsibility.

Then they blew up a Beaver Burrito, one of a hundred and ninety in the city, in the middle of the night, and that got people's attention. People here like their Beaver Burrito.

The theory then was that this was high-grade vandalism, the work of disaffected teens with resources and smarts, or maybe they had an agenda against Beaver Burrito, which had always courted controversy with its risqué item names and underdressed staff, and some thought maybe they even had it coming. A few kids with big backpacks had been caught on tape riding bikes and graffitiing the walls of a nearby viaduct just before. You could always blame the kids, and they did. Then for a week, nothing happened. Well, something happened, but it was unrelated.

That week Charles had asked me if I wanted to stay with them for a little while. It would be nice, she said, to have another body in the house, particularly with people out there blowing up buildings. I think she could tell that I had been badly speared by love and was obviously adrift and neither she nor I could be sure if I could make it back without bleeding out. Maybe, I thought, she simply didn't want that on her hands. That was care, I thought. I took it as a sign and said yes and that's how I moved into the casita in the backyard that overlooked the darkened window of the untouched old bedroom of my sort-of-ex. Every night when the house lights flicked out one by one I stood at my window and watched the darkened square where she once slept. Sometimes I gave in to memories and rubbed one out, I admit, but I always felt worse about it later, not that that had ever stopped me before. Considering a woman's bedroom window turned on something in me that I couldn't explain, like someone lowered the needle in a record groove I wasn't even aware I had.

Mostly it was good living with Sharon's folks, comfortable and domestic, like marriage might have been. The commute did not improve, but I could combine it with some work on my sponsored miles of road, and anyhow I was definitely saving money.

The new job at the Core Facility really was somewhere else, underneath the light and heat, in the darkened tunnels that couldn't be any less Arizona. It was better than walking down the rows of servers at the server farm, guarding heat and hums, which is what I had been doing. The new job was security, too, they said, though really it was wait and see, watch and handle animal intrusions, which came with surprising frequency. Try not to get outwitted by the badgers, they had said, as if there were any badgers in the state, or in retrospect perhaps that was a joke. Essentially the job was to adjust the dials that controlled the phalanx of supersonic hums we used to try to drive out the squirrels and the other critters. One hum would seem to drive an animal away or piss it off but have no effect on another. There was no pattern. So you had to adjust the hums constantly, cycling through the programmed stations.

I started blasting Rod Stewart on the speaker, which seemed to work more often than you would expect. I got it down so I'd do my little "Do Ya Think I'm Sexy" dance as I cued it up, and the squirrels would start to gather, and if I got lucky we'd all make it through to his cover of "Downtown Train," which was a sadder song than it seemed at first. If the spectacle of my dancing and the music didn't work I'd try to hit them with the shovel or whip them with a surplus SCSI cable that had a particularly wicked range.

You can see, perhaps, how the Core Facility offered me new challenges. Such as, I didn't say, trying to find exactly which tube Sharon's supercooled body was kept in, since, not being on the approved list, I was not an approved visitor. Luckily, the company did not remember me from my three attempts to visit her. For some reason their systems kept those logs segregated from the employee records. I wondered if I was the first to have not entirely aboveboard motives to join the staff. I gave everyone the side-eye in case.

I wouldn't have visited anyway once I'd seen how these visits went. The office was short staffed one day, so I had to guide an efficient-looking woman with a limp felt hat into the elevator and down into the tunnels and bring her to the tube that held her son, or what was once her son. I didn't say that last part. When I logged her in, I could see the story: that he had been here fifteen years, how at first there were six of them, the whole family coming in to see him in his preserved state. How it took less than a year for the group to give up and now it was only his mother who came. How she came once a week. How she still believed. It had been nine years since anyone else was logged in with her. How she held her breath when I pulled out the gurney that held the tube, maybe expecting some kind of change, I wasn't sure, and instead how it was the same. It's always the same, she says. I looked at her with what I thought was a sympathetic face, as we were instructed to do, and said nothing. At first that was fine, but the silence grew electric and uncomfortable and kept growing and this was why I was not fit for sales, I realized, and soon I felt I couldn't breathe in the face of her expectation, and so I finally said something and what I said was "I'm sorry."

"Sorry for what? What did you do? What do you know?"

"N-Nothing," I said back, and that was true. I had done nothing. Could do nothing. All of this was controlled by algorithm. I said I was sorry that there was no change, that what she had expected had not yet come to pass. She sensed an opening and continued to badger me. While we

were all trained for face service, as they put it, actually one-on-oneing
with a client was unusual for me. Mostly my days consisted of walking
from tunnel to tunnel through hums—another job with hums!—and
silence, taking readings, singing little songs into the microphones that
led to the supercooled chambers where the bodies were preserved.
Each chamber had a microphone into which you could speak or
sing or coo or whisper all your secrets to the dead. The thinking was
that, as with coma patients, perhaps there was a connection to be preserved by intimate human speech. The more intimate, the better, the
visitors were told.

What they were not told was that these messages were recorded. I
didn't find this out until a year into my employment, when they'd asked
me to splice and isolate and loop a couple of hundred samples from the
reassurances, as they were called. I'd bragged about my abilities with
software at the interview, and someone had made a note, my supervisor
Denise told me, and so this was an opportunity to use those tech skills,
a chance to move up and increase my investment in the company, and
vice versa.

I had assumed that the mics were there for the visitors, placebos to
preserve the semblance of connection, to ensure that they felt included
in the process, which was of course ongoing and costly, of pointless
preservation, but I was wrong: Denise explained that research did show
some lingering effects of consistent human speech on the cryogenically
preserved. As if it had some cellular effect. Like consciousness? I asked,
bedazzled. No, she said. But it was an effect! They weren't sure yet what
it meant, so specialists sorted through the recordings of the reassurances, what was said into the microphones, and spliced out reassuring
bits that would be looped and played daily to the clients in the absence
of visitors. It was hard, she'd said, to keep up with the visitations. You
probably noticed this since you're a keen observer, obviously, she said,
with a bit of a wink that even I, oblivious as I was to social cues, picked
up. Families and friends move and die. They have lives. They go on. With
the reassurances, we can be sure that the clients receive communication
in an ongoing and consistent manner. That's what we want you to do
today, she said. Screen these tapes and identify the reassuring bits. Edit
them down and save them in this folder. Have a good time, she said.

I loved doing this. What I heard, however, was not largely reassuring.
There were, to be sure, pretty overtures of love and support, the sorts of
things that you'd write on a Get Well Soon card. More often than not,

though, you'd get a voice rambling on to the client about the troubles and intrusions in their daily lives: *I was in the Fry's Grocery down in Tucson, you know the one on Speedway and Pantano, and I was in the checkout line, and the checkout girl, I know you don't call them that but what do you call them when the checker is a girl? At any rate the check-out girl was flirting outrageously with a man in line as his groceries, a depressing lot, frozen pizzas and chicken nuggets and wine coolers, not a vegetable to be seen, and the man was married, obviously, I saw his ring, and well you know me, I was never one to hold my tongue and I did not and things got rapidly out of control from there, you wouldn't believe what this little bitch* . . . and at this point I clicked that one off and flagged it for deletion.

The reassurances got sadder, though, when they edged into confessions, in which visitors unburdened themselves to the pretty-much-dead at length. I wonder if that helped, having a handset in which to speak, knowing that your words wouldn't go anywhere. Except of course they did, to me, their accidental confessor. I have to say I listened raptly.

These shook me. When I asked, Denise explained, pressing her hand down onto my shoulder and gesturing at the screen: the reassurances fell into several different sorts of language act. There were the confessions, the one-sided conversations, the expressions of anger and abuse, declarations of affection, stuff read out loud into the mic for no obvious reason, songs, and other. Code it using the chart, she said. Sometimes you'll need more than one code per message. And go back once you've coded those that you've flagged as appropriate and clip them down into loops of sixty seconds or less. It doesn't matter how much sense they make. I asked her: What do I do with the other stuff? She said just code it; recordings with the right code get deleted automatically every night. We can't save everything.

So here I was in charge of what the dead would listen to on loop, which messages got conveyed and how. Listening to one story someone was telling on the headphones, not a good one obviously, since I sort of faded out, I thought back to a story Sharon had told me that she had been told by this guy she was with on this caving expedition, like down in a cave for three days, no light no exit no nothing, and how spectacular that was, how it felt unlike anything else she'd ever felt, our whole relationship included, being there in the darkness and how you find the need to fill it, and on day three this guy, of course it was a guy, had told this story as they were camped out around their LED and their cold-

serve food packs about how he and a friend were camping in one of the
national forests north of here, up in the mountains, and they were pretty
high on mushrooms at this point (of course they were, I said to her), and
they were out wandering in the woods, his friend and him, and they came
across a gnome. A gnome? I said. Yep. They brought it back to the camp
and some stuff obviously occurred without their noticing it, and the next
morning they got up—sober now, or more sober now—and looked at
each other and the guy asked his friend, So did we find a gnome in the
forest last night? Yeah, his friend said. We brought it back. We gave it some
dog food since it seemed hungry. I don't know what happened then. And
they unzipped their tent and sleeping by the ashes of the fire there was
a kid, like a three-year-old. It turned out, as they'd find out later, that the
kid had been abandoned by his parent, or maybe parents, in the forest;
turns out that happens sometimes, especially with first-generation im-
migrants from certain other countries with kids who had special needs;
it was real fucking sad but it was true, which made it not racist, he said;
and fair enough, I guess; and they'd found the kid wandering and hungry
in the forest and thought he was a gnome and they had saved his life.
They'd brought him back and fed him and given him water, thinking all
the time they'd found a gnome and fed it, and they were heroes, they
were told eventually when they got back within cell phone range and the
cops came and took the kid. They were able to track down the parents,
and I don't know what happened after that, but the guys got citations of
bravery or valor or were otherwise compensated by the Forest Service or
were given lifetime passes to camp on national forest land.

I'm not sure why that story is the one that sticks with me of all the
ones Sharon told, but I think of it a lot, what it might have been like
for the kid to have been dropped off out there all alone, for who knows
how long, looking into the darkness, like it might have been fun for a
couple of hours, depending on the kid's disposition and willingness to
run around and hit shit with branches, but I think of the moment where
he must have maybe realized that this wasn't going to change, that this
was how it was now for him, just him out in the wilderness, and I can't
even follow that thought further without tearing up, and then I think
about the parents or probably *parent*, I'd imagine, it being harder to
imagine how two people could have come to this, and what that might
have felt like to them later, like what the shape of their guilt or shame
was, and what they must have felt they deserved when the cops showed
up in their driveway and carted one or both of them off.

The thing is, though, that people disappear in national parks all the time. There's this whole database of missing people that this guy Sharon knew had been putting together. He was writing a book about it, those gone missing in Park and Forest Service Lands, which he pointlessly abbreviated PFSL. For some reason, she said, they weren't counted with the regular missing persons by the police. And so there were no data on them anywhere, and people went missing more often than you'd think in national forests. Sure, I said, I could see that, getting lost or whatever. Or murder, she said, or abandonment. And so her friend was compiling all this data, calling all the parks and trying to document it and see what the data had to say. She was fascinated by this. She told me all about it as we cruised through one of the many unincorporated cities outside the highway rings that form the outer and theoretical outer-outer border of the Phoenix metro area. There might at most be a couple of buildings or something industrial or a gas station. They're called Census-Designated Places (or CDPs), and are populated but unincorporated, pre-towns, perhaps, not exactly within the law. She had a thing for driving through them, trying to understand something essential about Arizona that had given rise to so many CDPs. I think the one we were going through when she told me about her friend was called Wittmann. I only know this now because I looked it up, trying to cement its memory. Some stories seem to make a home in you, and asserted themselves when you were idle, I realized, and I wanted to remember where this one started burrowing, and I could thank Wittmann for that.

In life, Sharon had surrounded herself with these fringy friends, those who'd opted out of big parts of the culture because of how they looked or acted. It made for interesting and occasionally interminable party conversations, yes, but these were the sorts of people who most people weeded out of their lives. That she hadn't seemed like either generosity or inertia, and I wondered what that said of me.

The bombings didn't escalate so much as spread throughout the city apparently unplanned, like the city itself. Someone blew up a payday loan building that had recently been closed because payday loans had been outlawed. Another one—that now offered not payday loans but payday advances—sprang up right behind it, overseeing the ruins of the first. It took less than a month to clean, sort through, and recertify the demolition site for redevelopment. I watched it happen on my drive in and back each day. I followed its progress as the forensic trucks came and left and then the hazmat trucks came and left, and the tape came down and the hole was filled in, the contractor signs went up, the rubble got carted away to some godforsaken chunk of desert, and here it was, the new foundations and steel girders, the promise of another future, and then another business, and soon if you didn't know you wouldn't notice it had gone.

The group that claimed responsibility for this particular event called itself the Small Hand. They did it and would keep on doing it for reasons I forget. We are in your city, they wrote, among you all the time. That wasn't news, but the news reported it like it was. If you didn't know that the Core Facility was here, for instance, you'd have never guessed. The signage was unassuming—though it looked grand in its pyramid, the credit union down the street looked grander, an inverted pyramid twice as tall and half again as wide, even less architecturally viable. You couldn't drive by it without wanting to blow it up, I thought: how easily it would fall! The facade of the Core Facility had seen better days—the sun fades things fast down here—and so it gave no indication of the extent of the storage tunnels underneath the thing. So who knows what other secrets this city held? Most of Phoenix was this way. It felt like everything was concealing something: a terrible secret; a day care; a pyramid scheme; a crime scene; that this building had been built on Indian remains, cursed ruins, or irradiated ground. In fact, Terry had told me once, most of the companies based in Phoenix aren't even real. Eighty percent of the locksmiths, for instance, listed in the search engines in Phoenix don't actually exist. Companies pay, he explained, to insert fake images in the street view database so that a store appears where none exists. It's a redirected calling center to someplace elsewhere that will rip you off.

I wish I could say I was surprised but after Sharon's death nothing felt new to me. Most businesses didn't exist. Bombers were among us. Everyone who's here, I figured, came here to leave some wreckage behind: ripped-off relatives, angry customers, a spouse you killed and interred in a lake, lawsuits, disgruntled and impregnated student interns, just-healed stab wounds to the gut, who knows what. I'm not from here. Who is? So the prospect of bombers in the car behind me slowing to a crawl in traffic and sizing up my block, well, there was something about the city that sometimes made me want to blow something up too. Why had it taken them so long?

I clicked into the middle of a reassurance, someone dirty-talking to a client, and I had to rewind to locate the beginning since obviously I wanted to hear it all. What did it mean, I thought after superhot baby pussy this and oh oh oh oh fuck me daddy that, to dirty-talk the dead? I looked at the file to see if we had video, which we didn't. Did this count as reassurance? I filed it under "other." It got me a little hot, the thought of it more than the talk itself, I should admit, and I made a note of the locator code and took a break to cool down, avoiding Denise, since how do you talk about how you feel about something like that with your flirty supervisor?

Walking through the passages in the B wing of the Core Facility I was struck again by how intestinal they looked, how they weren't smooth and clean like you'd expect, but kinked and serpentine. The thought was that architecture from organic forms might have advantages, as Denise had explained, over space-age steel and glass and lines. The A wing was like that, all straight lines and glass, what we thought the future would look like fifty years ago, she said, and those in residence there skewed older. There were still spaces in A wing for those, though, but B wing had started to fill up. How do you want your future? they might as well have asked, when they asked A wing or B.

Sharon was B wing. It was cheaper and Terry and Charles both skewed a little hippie, in case it isn't obvious. Their home was filled with African carvings and beads and rugs. Charles had actually been in Africa when she was younger, she had explained, and brought a lot of it back with her. I believed the story because why not, but she didn't seem like the kind of woman who had gone to Africa. The four little elephant stools that came together to form a table were kind of beat up now, and the ivory on one of them had broken. There was no point in throwing that ivory away, she'd explained, when I asked, feeling transgressive for a change; I mean, she said, the elephants that gave their lives had already given their lives, and throwing the ivory away wouldn't change that. Really its display honored them. It showed that these elephants existed. In their way they did still, only as stools. You couldn't sit on them without thinking about what they used to be.

B wing was where the facility was running a long-term study to see if the architecture made a difference on the conditions of the clients. Maybe only one person really thought it would—I got that sense—but why not, everyone else had figured. The more research the company seemed to do, the more legit it appeared.

It took a little doing to figure out where Sharon's body was housed, and while I hadn't yet lit up the tube where she was kept, I now walked

by her on my rounds. You had to input a code to pull the screen back
and light the tube. The computer made a note of every tube that got lit
up for a visitor, and the lighting up of the tubes activated the recording.
Walking by her tube was as far as I had got with my obsession. I didn't
know if even I wanted to see her preserved in there. I mean, dead was
dead. Still I felt a little charge every time I turned the corner and saw her
number pass. I would slow my gait a bit, run my hand along the white
plastic of a cooling pipe, pretend to check an LED light or the numbers
on one of the adjacent tubes. They never changed.

The weird thing was that the gnome story didn't go away. I was at another
party—in spite of the bombings there were more parties; there were even
bombing parties with bomb-themed drinks. I thought it was in bad taste,
honestly, but others said it spoke of our resilience! And besides, parties were the only times I saw other people, really, except for Terry and
Charles, and so parties were how I marked the passing of time—and so
I'd go to them, and at one, someone else was telling the story. I was pretty
drunk by this point and into the lonely stage of the evening, even surrounded by people, and I walked into it. They were in a circle, the party
guests, or the ones who wanted to cluster outside. It was Terry telling it.
I watched people's faces open in disbelief. I watched them more than I
watched him. He'd embellished it with more details now about exactly
which drugs they had taken, and how high they were. The park had
changed: it was now on a mesa in New Mexico. And it was him camping,
now, out there, with these guys who brought back the gnome.
    I was overcome with disgust at these changes, the shift in ownership,
though I couldn't say why, it's not like a story's yours and yours alone,
especially when it's a spectacular one and you share it. So I had no
reason to feel the way I felt, I admit it, and when people started laughing
at the reveal I shot Terry one hard look before I walked away. He was
wearing a ring of their approval. I didn't know if he could read my face
then—or ever, really. But couldn't he see that the story's sad? I wanted
to tell him, to tell all of them, but didn't. I wanted to say that's your dead
daughter's story you're telling, but I guess it didn't matter because I didn't
say it after all.
    Instead I went to the firepit out back and warmed my hands on it. I
got my hands as close as I could to the fire without burning them, but
I could feel them heating up. I wondered: How long could I take it here
like this? I could hear them all behind me laughing and following up

with questions. The night was cold. From here you could see the little glow of far-off fires down the mountain somewhere. Maybe they were natural.

The bombings continued, though with even less effect. I couldn't always tell what had been bombed and what had been abandoned after a half-assed frenzy of development, so it was increasingly obvious that Phoenix was a poor choice as the Small Hand's primary target. You could track their escalating frustration that their work had not yet achieved paralysis, the desired effect. Even their story changed. First they were anticapitalist, then they were singing the many charms of Phoenix even as they blew it up. I followed them on Twitter. Their tweets became increasingly histrionic, railing against the perils of late capitalism and urban sprawl. They occasionally got into online fights about the hockey team that used to be the Phoenix Coyotes and was now the Arizona Coyotes and in a year wouldn't be anything at all, having moved to Las Vegas or Winnipeg or Oklahoma City.

The Small Hand wasn't wrong about late capitalism, but they underestimated the size and spread and resilience of the Phoenix sprawl, the sheer number of Beaver Burritos and our appetite for what they served. A Jack in the Box had to close because of the smoke. A body shop replaced a destroyed sign. Another Beaver Burrito—this one on Sunnyside, next to an elementary school—was blown up, and the space spawned another, and another: there were two, side by side, where there used to be one. Both did a brisk business, cars backed up into the street waiting to garble their orders into the drive-thru.

Some road was always closed, and cars moved off the interstate to the surface streets that also seemed to go on forever. Fires still burned in one of the sites, and then fires burned on several visible mountain slopes. They could not be put out; they could only sort of be contained. The statistics on the fires mentioned only the percentage containment and the sheer weight of resources—men and chemicals and machines—deployed to halt their spread. Still, the mountain fires were much more visible than the bombing fire, which, while it burned, was one hundred percent contained, there was no threat from it, and when we got our first monsoon storm it would be extinguished.

I followed the Small Hand's progress not only out of curiosity but also because it was something to track. I made maps. I put pins in them. I connected one to the next incidence with string. I kept waiting for a pattern to emerge. I had experience with patterns and explosions. When

I was younger—this was back in Michigan—my friends and I were obsessed with bombs. We'd blow stuff up out in the forest before it snowed: refrigerators and abandoned cars, mailboxes, mail, snowmobiles, televisions we'd found out back of the Goodwill. We'd make bombs from recipes handed down to us by older boys, our betters, those we'd have to seek to supplant if we wanted ever to make a mark on this place. Then it would snow and all of it—the bombs, the fires, the boys, the burn marks on our hands—would be erased.

It was only a matter of time before I started listening to Sharon's reassurances. You probably figured this out already. I guess it was inevitable—it seemed that way in retrospect—but it didn't feel like it at the time. It took an act of will for me to go that far. I'd been spending more time listening to and coding the reassurances, and they'd allowed me to start editing them and queuing them up too. With that responsibility came more access. With more access came more risk. What if they ran a background check now that I was deeper in the system? I caught Denise looking at me more attentively now that I had proved my worth. It was like she hadn't ever seen me before. I noticed her more too.

I still hadn't told Terry and Charles that I was working at the facility. I knew how they'd feel about it, creeped out probably, or else they'd pump me for information I didn't have, and it was easy enough to let them believe that I continued to work at the server lab. The work seemed about the same, and what was the difference, really? It was all maintenance and machines and passages and occasionally trying to kick a rat in the face but not succeeding. Since I almost never got to see the visitors, I had no fear of running into them there, and besides, Charles only came once a month for a while and then a year passed without her coming for a visitation. Terry came every two weeks without pause, and he spent more time in the tunnel, speaking into the handset, according to the logs. Most of what he said had been deleted by the time I got to it, but there were a couple of cached selections, one of him singing songs from the 1970s. They played those songs at home a lot: "Drift Away," "Desperado," the sort of songs you still heard sometimes on radio stations where they played old, sad songs to people too old and sad to understand that they were old and sad. Maybe they had always been that way, I thought, these listeners waiting for their chance to age into the role, to cocoon themselves in memory. Phoenix had a lot of these stations. They'd come in only intermittently as you came down through the mountains into the rings of freeways and new developments, speeding up to pass one car only to have the one you merged behind slow down pointlessly.

On account of the bombings I'd had to find new ways of getting to the facility, so I discovered new stations whose signals surged and took over the ones that I'd listened to before. I could be halfway through some trip-hop jam as I'd cross some invisible boundary from one domain into another, and suddenly I'd be filled with "You're So Vain," and before I realized it the song started to come true: I began to believe the singer was singing it about me. It started to almost feel like an augury, how one truth would intrude into another. In this way I learned a lot about the 1970s.

So when I heard the song it was obvious whose work it was: that voice was unmistakable, and of course I knew the songs, or some of them anyway. The editing was sloppy, so the loop was joined midsentence, with Terry saying something about how her room was the same, how not a thing was moved, how he wasn't sure if that mattered, how he didn't think she could hear him, and your mother, she's sorry she can't be here to speak to you, but she's so sad now all the time, and can't deal with the facility and how strange it was that you weren't aging, not really, and he was, how time collapses in moments like this, and then he broke into song.

I'd never heard his singing voice before. It was beautiful, I thought, if amateur. He was only halfway through the song when the loop cut out, or maybe he did, gave up and stopped and put the handset down. There was no click or sound of switching off. The recording kept on going on with silence. I flagged the loop in the system as Needs Attention, though I knew that just meant it would be deleted. Still, it seemed right: this recording needed attention, as did Terry, I didn't say. How alone was he now with his daughter gone?

I couldn't look at the screen for a while after that. I kept seeing this ring of light, like a lens flare or a little rainbow bull's-eye. It wasn't one of those things you see when you close your eyes. My eyes were open, I was sure of it, and the light was there. It did not track with my gaze. Maybe there was something broken in the screen. I wasn't sure. I felt stupid pressing my finger on it to see if it would smear, but I did, and it did not.

Then I felt a little tremor, like thunder, but subtler. I checked all the readings I could see. The lights were steady. Nothing appeared to have changed.

I got back to the control room and Denise asked me if I felt it too. I did, I said. She didn't know what it was. Was it something structural?

No, she said, it wasn't ours. We had sensors dialed into everything. There was a little blip, but it wasn't us, so it was something verifiable, but not something that needed our attention. I figured out its source shortly after, when I arrived at the Beaver Burrito to get lunch for Denise and me, and found it cordoned off and smoking with bits of paper napkins floating in the air. The police had sealed off the scene. I stood outside it for a while, staring at the television cameras. Each was trained on someone with a microphone illuminated by a light, telling a story. I wasn't shocked except that this was where I had meant to go, and now the place was gone. When the lights clicked off and the cameras got stowed away and the newspeople returned to their satellite-dished vans, only then did I get back in the car. Almost an hour had passed while I was watching. I had a dozen texts on my bedazzled phone from Denise, who was wondering where I was and if I was okay. I hadn't felt it buzzing in my pocket, evidently. I asked the voice recognition app in the phone where I could find the closest Beaver Burrito, and it kept directing me to the rubble in front of me. I told the voice thing that this was no longer a Beaver Burrito, and to find me the next-closest one instead, not the one on Sixteenth and Seventh but another, but it seemed to be confused. You're standing right in front of it, the application said. She (of course she had a female voice) asked: Do you need help going in? No, I said. I see where it used to be. She asked: You're searching for a Beaver Burrito? Yes, I am. I want another one, I said. She said: if you're having trouble, I can help you with your order.

Frustrated, I chucked the phone in the back of my car and went out to find another Beaver Burrito. It wasn't hard.

I had ordered up two Tejanos from the next-closest Beaver and had pressed myself into a booth to await their delivery, which could be a while because they were understaffed and Everything Got Cooked from Scratch as the slogan went, though that seemed to me patently false. Everything Got Cooked from Scratch Sometime Ago and Stood Ready for Assembly was more like it. They gave me a free drink, though no ice, you had to pay for ice, and told me to park it for a minute. I could see a guy sobbing in the next booth over and so of course I turned and surreptitiously watched. He was holding two action figures, one in each hand, and arranging them in poses: here one was breaking up with another one; here was one returning a box to the other with a tiny figure inside. He'd spend a couple of minutes adjusting their arms and hands and step back and look and cock his head and adjust again. He'd gasp when he got it right. He had something he was getting close to, I could tell, but I didn't get to see what it was because they called my name and so I rose to pick up my order, and then there was no subtle way for me to stay to watch without the burritos getting cold. Denise was expecting hers. I had been gone more than an hour now. The phone was surely filled with texts. I could have got up and gone right back to the Core Facility, I bet, if I hadn't then overheard a woman in another booth telling the story about their dad who had, while hiking the Appalachian Trail, found and fed a gnome.

Later I came back to blow the Beaver Burrito up, and afterward, as if in penance, I bagged all four miles of trash on Sharon's proposal road. They say you don't forget your first for a reason. It did feel different from the trash cans and rusted-out school buses we'd bombed back home. This wasn't abandoned: it was closed. I did check to make sure no one was there. I have lines I won't cross.

And it didn't go like in the movies I replayed in my head. I'd broken in with a centerpunch on the glass of the front doors, and kicked the glass outside the door so it looked like it had broken from within, then I fired up the gas on the whole row of stoves and let it run for as long as I could stand it, I wanted to make sure I smelled it and let it build, and I opened up the door and threw a road flare inside and snuck across the street and waited. All I heard for a while was a little *whump* and then a *flump* and I could feel the air get hot. But the windows didn't all explode out in a giant Death Star ball of flame. I was watching from a safe distance under the viaduct. I had a cold burrito in my hand, the one I had told Denise I'd eaten when I brought hers back, but I hadn't. I had kept it. I knew I'd be hungry later. It was like a switch got flipped and I'd leveled up, and these were times that you want to eat so you could get bigger. I couldn't stop eating. I'd even stop by another Beaver Burrito on the way home to buy another big one to sate me.

All the gas had done was start a fire, and it didn't spread fast enough. As I held up my phone to take a shot I saw the light and then there was what you could describe as something exploding. One window cracked, and I could hear the sound of breaking glass. I heard a voice shrieking what sounded like *Woo ha Woo ha* and cackling, though I couldn't see where it came from. I stayed there where I was, concealed. I didn't move for a half an hour to ensure I wasn't seen. I heard no sirens or flashing lights. She who cackled: What or who was she and where? Would she wait me out or flee? Had she already gone? I checked my watch. How long could I afford to stay before police arrived? An hour? A day? A year? Eventually I concluded whoever it was had cried out independently, that these were unrelated cries, or maybe it had even been me. They couldn't have seen me in my spot. No one could. I'd picked it well. I'd checked. So I got up and walked toward the car like I was meant to be here. Perhaps I was, I said, aloud. I was a member of a team, I said. It felt like I was chipping in, like I was part of the effort now. I drove away to get more food as I've discussed and then to clean my stretch of road.

By this point it was pretty far into the night. I had cleaned up down to the last mile. As I labored in the median picking up chunks—of what, melon? well, chunks of something—with the grabber and the spearer I contemplated silence. Though I didn't have a lot to say most days, still I listened to what everyone else said all around me. Here no one talked to me. Nothing was explained. There were no coded messages to force myself to ignore. It was quiet here in a way the city never was, not even the abandoned parts. I could see roughly fifteen miles down the slope as the little blips of light crept slowly uphill, blinking in and out around the curves. Every few minutes a car would fly by with its brights on and I'd have to avert my eyes. If drivers saw me I don't know what they thought. I thought: What was my story anyway?

I tied and tagged the bag. The animal skull I'd found didn't count as trash, I had decided, and so I would take it home. I could take it all home if I chose, throw it in the trunk and find a use for it later. I filled eighteen bags by the time I was finished. It was a lot of trash. Why was another question: Why did drivers cast off so much stuff? Couldn't they wait twenty minutes for an exit? Why was it so hard to take what you consumed home? And why, when you heard a story did you feel the need to tell it all over again to someone else? Couldn't you just let the stupid thing lie there at the party?

By the time I got back to the house I had about an hour to wash off in the outdoor shower whatever smells had stuck to me and turn the car around to get to work on time. Denise wasn't going to be there today, and I was assigned to the control room in her stead. I let myself into the main house to put an extra Tejano in the fridge for whoever'd want it later. Everything was quiet. I could hear the hum of the fan Terry ran every night to help him sleep. I typed the passcode into the security system to shut the whole thing off so I could come and go. The LEDs clicked from green to blue. Because of the fan sound I could creep around and often would while they both slept. I rinsed off the skull in the sink downstairs because who knew what was stuck to it, and as I creaked up to Sharon's old room I had the thought that both of her parents were curled up in their beds like gnomes. Where Sharon was she was sure not curled: all the bodies in the facility were stood up vertically. I'd finally seen my first a week ago. A boy, Denise showed me, seventeen, motorcycle accident, no helmet, skull trauma. As such you couldn't see his face in his tube. The tubes had bands they'd install where appropriate for modesty, of course, and to keep visitors from seeing how bad it was. So instead of seeing the wreck of his head, the foot-long band displayed a digital image of his face. They're sourced from photographs, she explained, breathing a little fast. I'm not supposed to show you this stuff, she said, but you've been here long enough. That's why the image appears to move slightly as you change the viewing angle. Weird, I said. More than that, she said: it's superweird the first one that you see. I asked her: Could I see the actual head? How bad was this guy gone? Unfortunately, she said, that was restricted to the medical team. Even she couldn't access it except in the description in the file: the brain was only half there, she said. But what was there might be rebuilt, the theory went; documented cases showed that the brain could reroute almost any aspect of its functionality. I asked: I mean, couldn't we just remove the band if we really wanted to? You could, she said, but you'd compromise the preservation. Oh, I said, that's cool. I'm just curious. I know, she said, and winked.

I wasn't sure what this was becoming between us, Denise and me, but it was starting to mean something different from what it did before. She'd asked me if I was single a while back and yes, I said, well, there had been someone in the picture, but she was gone. Or maybe I was, I thought. She asked: Like out of the story or out of the frame? I said all the way out. What doesn't fit in the frame doesn't fit in the picture. What we'd had was ruined, I'd said, and it was no one's fault, and I was over it. Which I wasn't, obviously, not entirely, working here, but nobody wants to hear that. So I courted Denise's attention. I brought her lunch and little gifts, like origami horses I'd pose and leave on her station.

Partly they installed the clients upright because it was aspirational, she said, to give you the sense that at any moment they could stride right out of their supercooled tube and drape their arms around you once again. And that's why I knew Sharon or what she used to be was upright in the B wing, dreaming no dreams. I wasn't sure why I cracked open her parents' door: I'd done it before, but it felt a little new now, and I watched them for a moment, sleeping, curled away from each other, as I said. I could have gone in and stood over them but I didn't. I did think about it. I closed the door and backed down the hall. I went to Sharon's room instead and put the cleaned-up skull underneath her pillow. I didn't know what kind it was (maybe an opossum?) but it was cool and smooth, not white like you'd think: more a spotted gray, like it'd been out there for a while, getting chewed on by the world. I don't know, in retrospect, why it was I did this either. I felt charged up, like anything I touched I could electrify. I went back downstairs, took that shower I mentioned, masturbated thinking of things I don't want to reveal, clicked on the local television news to see if there was coverage of the latest bombing, which there wasn't, and meant to stay awake but fell asleep.

I got to work late as a result, which took some explaining. The facility counted this against me, I was told. No problem, I said. I was a new man. I wouldn't be late ever again. I was on control all by myself for the first time. They sent the temp controller home and I slid—I slide, rather, always in my memory this is enacted in the present tense—into his seat, still warm from his perspiration and body heat. He looked a little like a cartoon animal, I thought, as he walked away.

Was this the place where my proposition had gone awry? I asked this of myself, back in the sub-basement control room where we could monitor all the signals from all the machines making sure the dead stayed dead, or stayed preserved, which was as close to alive as we could manage. Maybe that's all we could ever do: keep time at bay.

Here all the signs converged, though they almost never changed. I sat there looking at the lights. A number tinked from .4 to .41 and tinked right back. I stared at it. It was a composite, not a single reading, so I didn't know for sure what it meant. I took a note. That's what I was here to do. The big screen had a thousand readings. Were we safe? We were, I thought, safer than anywhere else I could imagine. The whole place was built to withstand a nuclear strike, I learned in my second week here, because A wing was a nuclear bunker. This was important to a subgroup of our clientele: the sort who believed in sleeping in barometric chambers and amassing guns and that the federal government could do no good not ever. Originally we were so far out of the city that this was seen as a safe distance for the moneyed cognoscenti to seek shelter. But we were out of the city no more. It kept expanding until we were in it. No one knew it was here: that was the point. I knew from scheduling how long I would have, where security went on their rounds and how long they took, and so I bided my time there.

So you know I found my way into the B wing where Sharon's body was. This meeting was, I told myself, inevitable. Something had to change, and something did, and now something else would change too. Ever since you were taken from me, I murmured to the screen, I knew we would meet again, even if in this diminished way. It wasn't that I was stuck in my old patterns of grief, I wanted to say: I've moved on. That's what I was here to say, that I had shed that skin. I was something different now: emptied. I entered the authorization code and the screen slid up—what was this? a peep show booth?—and there she was, cool and blue and hairless, silver in the tube. She was suspended from behind on some kind of plastic hook that also fed her veins. I knew it was there but could not see it. She was naked but bands concealed what you would want to see if you were me. I remembered well enough, and so what if one breast got sheared off in the accident and was now a memory of what it used to be? I am here, I said. I know this is not for you, I said. I asked her: What was the point of saying anything to the dead? Who were you anyhow? How much of you was there I didn't know?

I watched her lips as best I could, and felt foolish afterward for hoping. I opened up the side panel to see if there was any sign of change. I thought I felt another tremor, but nothing on the readout told me that was true. For a second I thought she might wake and chide me that life is not a fairy tale and tell me that was it, that was my problem, or if not that, then something was. Or tell me that what I would have to give to get her back I could not give, not now, not ever, and that was why she had said no. Or tell me anything, really.

She looked so beautiful and still, still beautiful, like she was capable of anything, of living again, even, and this is about as close as you're going to get to a confession, I told her then and I'm telling you now. All of it is just a story, I said, in case I was being surveilled or overheard. I know it's just a story, I said. But I believe it's something more, something you were telling me, something the world's still telling me. I asked her: Is it even yours? I know it is a test, a self-diagnostic, like the kind we run on the systems here, the kind that never fails. Every time I tell it, it takes ahold of me anew. And I keep asking myself, I said into the microphone: Am I the high guys in the forest or am I the gnome?

In a Structure Simulating an Owl

My invention relates to a structure simulating an owl. The object of my invention is to provide a structure simulating an owl as an article of manufacture. A further object of my invention is to simulate an owl as an ornamentation. A still further object of my invention is to provide a structure flexible in part and being colored simulating an owl.
—Grace E. Wilson, United States Patent Office
Application 531,317, filed April 20, 1931

1. In a structure simulating an owl in which are inscribed the eyes of my former husband, etched on shook silver foil, serving as a replica of his eyes in his absence, blue dashed with bits of white as if they were in every moment on the verge of dissolving into a simulacrum of eyes, all of us being simulacra, I have been feeling recently, of ourselves from former moments, indistinguishable (as is the way of simulacra) from what others, even our lovers, our husbands, our dream-sons, our conquerors, our makers, might identify erroneously as ourselves when seen from a distance or even up close if approached quickly enough, in the way that the self can usually be described as two sheets of thin metal folded four or more times and in some complex cases many more (a machine may be required to create this effect) and pinned together by a small bolt, fastened eventually by a nut, the entirety of my history may be included in or referred to by a succession of small moving parts.

2. In a structure simulating an owl in a dream I have had every year on this date, as far back as my memory goes, in which I am in my father's workshop, a word that was among my first (*workshop*, not *father*— though the two are conflated now in my memory), watching him from a very great distance, which is of course in this structure not geometrically

possible except in dreams, as he works above a burning-hot woodstove shaping some kind of metal, at which point I kick over a bucket of what must be kerosene or some burnable liquid that spills onto the floor where a rope is somehow soaked in fluid, and it is only moments before the rope connects to my father and a number of unidentified canisters and I have no language with which to warn him since as quickly as I try to speak my voice is stuffed with cotton swabs and my breath is fire and my warning turns to flame along with everything in the workshop including my father and his eyes, which in every photograph remind me of owls, a human or a memory of a human may be for some time ensconced.

3. In a structure simulating an owl in which I have been making something for the world that might, in a small way, change it, so as to have an effect on something for once in my life, since I have been recently feeling as if I were a ghost, some combinations of my dreams and waking life and my many so-called sins will be made manifest at last.

4. In a structure simulating an owl composed primarily of wire and sixteen separate moving pieces designed to spark terror in all creatures preyed on by owls if they come within sight of said structure as it is attached to a post by a rivet or a wishing screw, six feet or higher above the ground, and in some cases it might be suspended from an outdoor ceiling fan or from a series of wire loops attached to a belt-driven mechanism activated by the lack of light so that it moves in an elliptical fashion and makes a sound somewhat like an auk makes, an onomatopoeia, a word I have wanted to use since I was twelve and discovered it in the oldest dictionary available in the public library where I spent my days fingering through pages, in which I learned one might describe one's life or another's by words, not exactly shunned by my peers but hardly invited out, and not engaged in any official after-school activity though I did have tendencies toward delinquencies, breaking into the school bus factory a mile down the road from home to sit in the unfinished buses, lonely, my father dead, my younger brother years dead already, dead almost before I knew him, having died when he was two and I was five, my older brother absent, gone somewhere that I could not access, and on these buses I would carve my name with his or with other boys' and sometimes girls' in the backs of the vinyl seats, licking all the places where I knew someone's hands might touch in the bus when it would be eventually finished, deployed, and driven, possibly even on the route that terminated

at my house after passing the place of its manufacture, an irony lost on machines and on the drivers of machines and on the many other hands and eyes that resulted in these machines and touched these machines and their sale and deployment on this route, this date, in which they might catch a glimpse in the dying light of the outline of an owl on a high post or possibly moving through the air and wonder what it was in the approaching dark, or thrill perhaps at the fact of owls with their moving parts and soundless flight and outstretched arms that might in another life have entwined with my own, I might find some satisfaction.

5. In a structure simulating an owl, it is incontrovertible that I have been in some way seeking transformation.

6. In a structure simulating an owl my marriage might be seen closely enough through the attached range finders built into the structures simulating eyes, so as the marriage might appear real, not simply as described by law, but in the hearts of both partners legally obligated to each other for the rest of their lives until dissolution or death, a statement neither my husband nor I took lightly at the time, though as with all infinities, or seeming infinities, their true extent is inapprehensible, barely even glimpsable from the moment in which a marriage can be made and committed to, and from that particular location in which the structure simulating an owl might be placed, one might see over time the way that marriage decayed, due in no way to the behaviors or intentions of the couple but because of the ways a domestic life can drive a couple apart like a lead wedge placed in a crack and hit with a heavy sledge with a lifetime's worth of force, re-sulting in approximately two structures that, when held side by side and looked at together, formerly simulated an owl.

7. In a structure simulating an owl one's life might be understood in retro-spect, from its very last chapter, as a series of actions and reactions, chemi-cal, biological, emotional, metaphysical, all collected together and held for a moment by the mind, and therein might be seen a method to it at last.

8. In a structure simulating an owl, as the present invention proposes to demonstrate, each moving part or pin being constructed of lines on paper in attached diagram 1, if looked at closely enough with a scan-ning microscope, one might note that the lines are not solid lines but scattered ink on paper, not corporeal parts at all, as if to say a physical

thing might be actually enacted and made to move and apparition as an animal, we might be in this way terrified by it as we are when woken suddenly enough with enough force.

9. In a structure simulating an owl, as all structures start to appear if you look at them long enough and hard enough, as if they were one of those magic-eye 3-D drawings that only the annoying are apparently able to see, you will see the future of the owl or really the structure simulating it combined with your own future as manifested in your actions; this outcome is what creates the necessity of the forty-four levers that work behind the metal outer skin of the structure to create the illusion of the owl, though if you were, say, an owlet, or another interested owl it's probably plenty obvious that this structure only simulates an owl in name and shape, and in some of the motions of its wings, not in the scent of an owl, or the way an owl actually flies, meaning that while a structure simulating an owl might simulate an owl it cannot fully be an owl: as long as we understand each other then we can communicate.

10. In a structure simulating an owl that is equipped with increasingly verisimilitudinal scent glands one might secrete the sorts of scents that might fool another owl, a slow one, for a second, and in so doing, could one actually be considered an owl for a moment, which is to say can a sufficiently advanced illusion be a kind of magic?

11. In a structure simulating an owl that does not account for the amorphous quality and (both wonderful and not) unpredictability of love, and the effect of its loss and slow replacement by the love of another, an impossible love, really, in many ways, not possible, surely, to admit out loud or in writing or in the presence of anyone, ever, if you value your marriage and the pleasing domesticity that it brings, along with the overly alliterative, you understand, damningly dull domesticity that drives me in moments out to the workshop where, in my own world of wire and awl and dictionary and hammer, I can immerse myself for days in the process of producing a structure simulating an owl.

12. In a structure simulating an owl I might more easily understand the ways in which I have transgressed, and another structure simulating an owl might be understood to move of its own volition and driven by its own internal mechanisms, however obscure, containing my estranged husband,

who I thought understood how I worked and what drove me to do what
I did, but who refused to make allowances for my strange behavior in the
last two years, though he said he tried, goddamn he did, he said, and I
believe from this distance that he did, he did the best he could, and some
things end eventually, it's physics, sure, entropy and all, our bonds are only
temporary, and in this guise surrounded by this nest of wire I can get some
distance from my former self and see history from hundreds of feet above
as if aloft and hunting for meaning in the motions of rodents.

13. In a structure simulating an owl ever more closely in this iteration,
the machine of one's life can be worked out, becoming an increasingly
fine construction of said structure, and shown to the ones one loves in
hopes of expressing the inexpressible in the absence of other ways we
might show our love.

14. In a structure simulating an owl that entrances animals if they come
within 140 feet of it, the cache of stored scents is released in response
to various stimuli that in the wild prompt owl-like behavior in owls, because all of us are creatures that respond to stimuli, I am finding in my
life and trying to make manifest in the world this fact, because given the
collective behaviors of people I come into contact with on a daily basis
who try to cloak their animal natures, as if they posit that they are not
animals, not entirely in command of their own urges, that they are not
like zombies, craven and driven to their desire, but that they are, like my
mother claimed to be, entirely self-aware and in full control of her facul-
ties so much that her resistance to every desire became a manifesto, a
way of living, a clothing that she wrapped herself with every day of her
life and would occasionally deploy to asphyxiate her children and her
husband: quite obviously it crushed her after years so that you had the
feeling that there was no inner sense of self, of what she would do if
freed from her own restrictions, since she said, for instance, that civilization means denying every desire you have in your filthy hearts, and if we
do not police our weaker moments, we are not human, and in this way
she became like a structure simulating a paragon or a structure of beliefs
in which she was housed, in which she might have hidden some small bit
of herself if it was possible to pull the whole thing apart, and that by this
lifelong simulation she was making some point to the world, and so even
when she was freed, her parents deceased, her husband deceased, all of
her other children deceased and just the two of us remaining she might

have been free of this, I hoped, and to that end I dosed her several times with psychotropic drops rendered from mushrooms gathered from her own front yard just after a storm, theorizing that it might jolt her into an uncomfortable former shell of herself and she might be forced to fight her way back into the present and what had become of her life: a hollow. Of course this was not possible because until her actual dying moment she persisted in simulating what she had always hoped or meant to be, and apparently became, to all of us who knew her and her seeming capacity to suffer endlessly, that she could absorb almost anything: all those deaths, sometimes two at once, an alcoholic son, a straying and promiscuous daughter, the decline of the world into a den of iniquity, if that's not saying too much in her own words, or what should have been her words if she was given to those sorts of proclamations, which she was not, which resulted in silence, which is the usual result of most stimuli to a structure simulating an owl.

15. In a structure simulating an owl having a flexible covering made primarily of hammered tin adorned with artificial feathers, one might spend one's days perched on one of a hundred points I have indicated on the attached maps, these points offering a particular vantage toward a particular view of, for instance, among the crowd of beasts released from school at 2:25 in the afternoon, the sun just so in the sky, my own son rushing out to his father's home which is exactly four kilometers from my own, the separate domiciles due in some small part to my own eccentricities, I have come to understand too late, resulting in loneliness and what is commonly referred to as my breakdown, though I saw it as a kind of reboot, a transformation, a shedding of an old skin, from a structure simulating a woman into an entirely new simulation, a pause followed by a subsequent burst of energy resulting in long spans of time spent in my own workshop—and oh!—from this distance they resemble a spray of pressurized water forced out of a crack that might eventually break open and let the whole tank crash onto the ground, or, perhaps better, a spread of mice fleeing some hole in which they had been pent up, and in their flight they might easily be snatched up by a creature of such size and floating grace and powerful eyesight such as a structure simulating an owl.

16. In a structure simulating an owl one might spend one's time roosting on the edge of the gargoyled roof of the bank building at the center of downtown, contemplating the stuffed insides of the creatures who spend

no time considering their own stuffings, the meat parts that make us up
and make the machine of the body work, the bland tours of glands, the
orifices and labyrinths, the complications of our systems, our bodies all
being flexible machines for digestion and peregrination and the slow
operation of our intelligences, grinding as they do toward a conclusion,
like the construction of these carved stone gargoyles, originally meant to
frighten off evil spirits, though they now mostly frighten the occasional
child whose gaze strays skyward to the perch and is justly startled by the
visage of these devilish creatures perched here, watching, waiting, thinking,
reserving judgment for the moment, planning decisive action alongside
a structure simulating an owl.

17. If the girl child were to point toward the structure simulating an owl
gleaming in the midafternoon sun, she might not understand that the
gleam is a result of three sets of interchangeable lenses that can be used
to focus and redirect sun into a steady beam that might transfix the
object of the structure simulating an owl's gaze long enough to distract
said object and to forever hold her there, as if in a sufficiently elongated
moment the structure simulating an owl might pass to the object of its
strange affection some kind of wisdom about what it is to be a woman
in the world buffeted as we are by the actions of those around us, constantly desired or stared at, starred and asterisked in the dreamlives
of yearning others, so that it is impossible to look at oneself without
the sense of being dreamed of or gazed upon, creating a doubleness, a
structure that starts, after a time, to simulate the self and that might be
mistaken for the self if the user is not careful.

18. In a structure simulating an owl either wisdom or killing is a natural
outcome of an interaction, owls being understood to be in possession
of some otherworldly wisdom, and owls being the instrument of killing,
and sometimes these two things being indistinguishable or interlocking,
a difficult fact to communicate.

19. In a structure simulating an owl one must necessarily be conscious
of wearing a mask.

20. In a structure simulating an owl one might be cold except for the
layers of insulation machined initially from gloves purchased at the local
Target, and then, after the initial trial run with these layers of repurposed

material, the prototype was fitted with up to six layers, depending on the climate you foresee operating in, of asbestos procured from India, though made and exported from Canada, a country that continues to ship asbestos to India in spite of what is known about its carcinogenic qualities, because economic growth is understood to be a universal good, and because an industry operating efficiently gains its own inertia and cannot easily come to a halt, and because warmth is of utmost importance while on location because in a structure simulating an owl it is very difficult to move, except by wire and servomotors.

21. In a structure simulating an owl one has dreams and must acknowledge those dreams as what they are: shadows of desire, the product of overlapping selves and biological imperatives and parental wishes and possibilities for lives understood from obsessive reading of magazines and many series of pseudonymous teen mysteries in which those who wear masks are uncovered.

22. In a structure simulating an owl I always dreamed—or even thought, assumed, as if a destiny was an inevitable thing, as if there was a such thing as a destiny, as if it could be understood except from the past tense, as if our lives could be seen just from beyond the point of our departures into nothingness or ever-afterness—I would be Miss Minnesota when I grew up, in spite of what I full well knew and was often told was evidence to the contrary: my nose overly sloped and unattractively hooked, my gait awkward, my arms overlong and even, as I was teased, resembling wings, and my gaze uncomfortably intense, not that I would be stopped from begging my mother to enter me in pageants from a young age. I'm not sure why exactly I wanted this so badly—perhaps it was a response to my father's death, in retrospect, and needing some way to cast a long shadow, as I did walking at night in the old neighborhood when the floodlights from the neighbors' houses would click on at my sudden movement, moving toward their windows and the lives I so desperately wanted to see and understand, as if by understanding their lives I could understand my own, and if at the proper angle the light would cast a shadow that would go on for over a hundred feet until I could no longer tell where there was shadow and where there was just darkness, and my wanting of this brilliant pageant dream increased in proportion to its impossibility, like the lover I fell for so hard that it finally split the structure simulating a marriage apart, in spite of that

long love spent with my husband, who had and has his faults, and one
of them was that he was powerless to stop my drift, geologist that he is,
knowing something about continents and their barely perceptible shifting, I would have thought he would understand this better, and I drifted
through those pageants in my mask, my makeup face fixed in a dazzling
smile that I would later reassess in light of what I had come to learn, in
short that by my not varying the smile people found me terrifying, spec-
tral really, as if I were not a woman but a mannequin, posed, smooth, but
somehow breathing, and this was one in a long string of revelations about
the ways in which I have misconstrued others' responses to the way I
conduct myself socially, spending weeks poring over etiquette books and
practicing responses to common queries to make myself more charming,
but in a structure simulating an owl you don't need these things to move
or see or appear or terrify a creature at a hundred paces, which may be
inevitable anyway the longer we live.

23. In a structure simulating an owl I will have receded successfully from
my life, my lives, both before our split and after, finally if not irretrievably,
so that I will have no appearance of my own, no face to terrify, no family to
be judged or misunderstood by, and in so simulating an owl in said structure for such a long time, in the view of others anyway, and as such in my
own view, since we do internalize the way we are considered by others
in our self-imaginings, I will eventually be transformed, and become not
just a structure simulating an owl or a woman or a woman simulating
an owl but something else entirely.

24. In a structure simulating an owl I will hope to understand—nay, I
will manifest—the desire I have read about in others and seen for myself, such as in my older brother's drunken state before he died when
he would tell me about what he wanted most deeply but never had the
courage to achieve, the desires of those who sexually fetishize amputees
(acrotomophiliacs), or, in more extreme circumstances, who desire to be
amputees and who might even undergo voluntary amputations (apotem-
nophiliacs), who feel their limbs are somehow wrong, too long, incor-
rect, or simply not a fit for them, who may have some version of body
dysmorphic disorder, but regardless, want what they want, as humans—
animals—do and good luck telling them not to want those things, in that
in this structure I might understand that transformation, even if it isn't
sexual for me as it was for my older brother, a fact he would not admit to

sober, certainly, one reason he was not often sober, that he once said, "I will never feel truly whole with legs," though he never had them removed, a fact he called a tragedy, and maybe it was a tragedy, not to get to live one's deepest-held desire, no matter how bizarre or increasingly frustrating or pointless, but maybe it was a sensible tragedy, given the extremity and oddness of his desire, and the ways it might have transformed his life—he knew it then, and he said as much, that it might have changed something in the world, in him, certainly, if we can change ourselves, which I desperately hope we can in my better moments even as I am not sure I believe it in my darker ones, though I will not stop trying, not ever, in whatever structure or set of clothes or metal exoskeleton I am currently working on—when he died last year, the final straw, as my husband said, ever cruel, overcruel, my mother was the one who cleaned out his home at his behest and when I asked her about the computer and what was on it, trying not to suggest I knew his secret or that he even had such a secret, trying to honor this luminous and folded place that he held within him, that I might have been the only one who knew, that I was wondering what sort of pornography he might have on there, she was of course circumspect, as she always is, and deflected the question, suggesting that she was another keeper of his secret, one he trusted more than me, given her lifelong goal of full-on repression of our other, darker selves, a fact I took as blame for not going far enough with him, a fact I am hoping to convert to a new understanding of what it might mean or be to become someone else—to become someone else—by silence, by patience, by devious mechanical engineering, and by sheer belief in a structure simulating an owl, to somehow become an owl.

25. In a structure simulating an ow! I mean an owl but was cut off midthought and midword in fact by the sight of something swooping in the darkness from this vantage point and that I was transported by its efficacy, I will dream again not as human but as owl—featherlight, meat-finding, unthinking—for a time.

26. In a structure simulating an owl I will remain at one of my designated posts no less than one year, removed from life, but not from vision, subsisting on what I can catch and eat, having studied this problem and the many hunting methods owls have and also foraging with my human hands where they extrude from the structure, perhaps in the gardens of my extended family and friends, wondering if they will have forgotten me

in a fit of self-protection or if they have written off my selfish exit, or if they are wondering exactly what an owl—what they will misapprehend and is in fact a structure simulating an owl—or perhaps it is an owl, thus the power and point of the extended simulation—might be doing in their backyard at night peering with its set of magnifying lenses into their windows, into their lives, and apprehending the resulting spaces that opened up in there, how they react, how they close and fill those spaces.

27. In a structure simulating an owl I do not expect to die.

28. In a structure simulating an owl I will hereby attempt to know the unknowable.

29. In a structure simulating an owl I will not live as I lived before, in guilt and repression—or in fully giving in to my baser urges and the corresponding renunciation of my former life—lives—and need for light.

30. In a structure simulating an owl in which a complex optical mechanism allows the use of infrared and ultraviolet light to augment and aid perception, an occupant or user can approximate the night vision of owls.

31. In a structure simulating an owl I cannot be my brother nor my father, nor my long-dead younger brother, nor my child, nor my husband, but I can also not be myself for a year or longer, and in so doing I submit that this invention will be revolutionary and of a deep and abiding effect for certain persons who want to live in what we refer to as a civilization—and occasionally retreat from it via engineered and exceptionally complicated mechanisms like this, in which we might be transported into another self.

32. In a structure simulating an owl the user might take that transfiguration even further and, by isolation and the fact of one's own diminishing humanity, more bodily embody these transformations into others such as owls.

In testimony whereof I affix my signature,

This Time with Feeling

Air comes through the window, flowing haphazardly through the house because gases will always equalize pressure in any container, and the house is a container like any other. The gases do their thing, which is to expand and whirl, molecules clanging off each other and heating up throughout the house, rising and cooling and failing back toward the world and repeating.

All the din is because the windows are open—bottle rockets whining through the night en route to nothing, proving something to the day, Lucia supposes. A bottle-breaking sound; "Shit yeah!" shouted loud. It's night and it's hard to see outside with the light on, so Lucia keeps it off in the front window through which she's looking. The windows are open to allow more air circulation through the top floor of the house via an elaborate fan system, all plugged into one surge protector, plugged thereafter into a clapper mechanism, the kind she once saw advertised on television that switches on and off in response to the sound of human hands clapping. Unfortunately, whenever two bottle rockets go off close to one another, the system shuts off, or comes on, and the electrical surge dims the rest of the house lights momentarily and you can see the surge even from outside. When this happens, Lucia thinks she can even see the slight glow of the streetlights dim and return. Periodically she fears that the douchebags have figured out the clapper mechanism and that they time their rockets to go off together to make the lights sway off and on in her house. She adjusts the timing on the mechanism so that they must readjust. This is a game of breaking codes: her against the neighborhood.

When the air moves around her body, Lucia is cool enough that she can stand it, but when the fans switch off it is another story. And the system goes on and off as flying objects trail through the night and explode.

In this way she has ceded control to the douchebags. She will not, however, give up her system.

Lucia is a woman. Women disappear all the time. The douchebags are responsible. She knows the names of some from occasional bouts of television: that show that always features murdered or kidnapped girls, white girls, usually beautiful and present on the screen, made up to please someone in their lives, made up and filled out now to please the viewer. They looked at the camera that had shot the photo, eyes locked toward the future, maybe imagining themselves a decade from now doing important work and looking back at their digital collection of photographs featuring themselves looking lovely and alone. Not picturing the future of them missing, murdered, suicided, maybe, but dead or on the way to dead, or failing that, completely disappeared. These girls are beautiful in contrast to their desperation: they are hoping to become icons, she thinks. They know how to behave in society. They believe in the norms we agree to share until we don't. They dress and eat and listen to each other on the telephone. These are learned behaviors. These girls have almost surely learned them well. This is why they are missing and on television. Each one of them is like a trophy on the screen, proof of something. The woman on the show missing the missing woman is angry, preaching almost, talking to another angry person or an implied angry person, or occasionally a woman weeping or a woman looking resolute: it's as if these are the only kinds of women.

These shows make Lucia angry. And then sad. And then she doesn't know how to feel about them. It is impossible to turn them off, until she does, and the screen blacks out, and she wonders why she was watching them, and hours have passed in this way. Is it living that she's doing?

It's hot out. Soon it will be Independence Day, and the world is alive in hopes of declaring a new freedom or celebrating an old one. Kids' shrieks perforate the night as they blow up trash cans or mailboxes or what sounds increasingly like big, hollow dumpsters all along the street—*boom, boom, boom*—she can hear the douchebags almost constantly, like it's a celebration or a punishment for her string of losses— and Lucia is staring out the window and angry and thinking about her past. She is always looking out. She is barely here now, she feels, sometimes, except as an eye, always open, turned outward, a satellite dish, a huge antenna. She is the neighborhood watch because who will watch the neighbors otherwise. Others appreciate her reports on their behalf. They tell her all the time, or they mean to. Her repeated complaints got the drug dealer up the block evicted though he left behind his two pit bulls who, alone for three days prancing in their own filth and hunger, burst through the window and screen and ran through the neighborhood, terrifying other dogs and freaking out and prompting calls to animal control. They got sprayed by the skunks from the colony down in the cul-de-sac just past the ravine, which made them even wilder. Lucia was one of the first to call the number to bring out the van with the men and cages and nooses on poles to take those dogs away to be put down.

Lucia is alone, though she isn't lonely. She tells this to her few remaining friends and the rare relatives whose visits and calls dot her days and fill her communication logs. Surely she is independent, her friends tell her, how lucky she must feel to be free and to be alive. These things are true and they are usually enough, she says.

She was once a physicist and learned to see the world in quantitative terms: strong and weak interactions, ionic and covalent bonds. Between people you see a number of different kinds of bonds. They act over great distances. They even—so she posits privately—work across the boundaries of the seen world and the unseen one that hides behind us all the time. Right now she is thinking of herself in the third person like an omniscient narrator connecting pushpins with string on a corkboard, and how she is in relationship to everyone who has come into and out of her life. It is easy for her to lapse into this kind of thinking.

Hers is a dwindling family thanks to a chain of suicides and accidents that might or might not have been suicides. She wonders what this says about genetics. She's down to one first cousin and two nieces, none of whom she is close to. All her male relatives have passed away, most recently an uncle who blew most of his face off with a shotgun on his first attempt but did not then die. He later claimed he was driven to it because his wife had left him, though later it would be obvious that she only left him after he blew most of his face off with a shotgun and, worse, survived. After that he must have required a lot of care, and when he talked it didn't sound like anything she had ever heard before. Tubes, bandages the size of handbags, silence, and the slop and drip of feeding—and the fear, of course, that, now disfigured, life would not improve, and he'd finish the job sooner rather than later. Lucia had always thought his wife was cruel, but she didn't blame her for leaving a month after incident number one.

He had returned the shotgun to Walmart for a gift card, no longer trusting himself with the instrument of his disfigurement around the house. This was a transaction Lucia wished she could have seen, as he explained the bandages and the gun to the customer service manager who patrolled the registers at night (it must have been night because, after, he would only go out at night, lurking from streetlight to streetlight like some kind of romantic monster). How awful to telegraph your story, but then, she figured, everybody did.

The second attempt was with a bomb—he called in the threat to another Walmart, the one where he worked, while he was working (from the employee phone as it turned out), but no one took it seriously. This was against company policy, he was sure, which they would realize when it went off, taking him and the refrigerator that held the employees' lunches with it, mixing them in a sort of batter spread all across the room. Except that it didn't go off. Botched wiring, and as he was bending over it in the break room with the huge smiley face etched on the glossy vinyl-covered concrete floor, ready to be walked all over like all things that smile without ceasing, someone saw him tinkering with wires and called security, and he was Tasered and tackled and maced a couple of times just to be safe and then Tasered again and then removed, subjected to a variety of treatments that he was henceforth reluctant to talk about.

The third time was enough to get it done. Shotgun number two, a second take, this time with feeling and a larger gauge, and with that he was done with the world, and vice versa. Walmart again, and if it seemed like a year later to the day that probably seemed to most like a coincidence. Biorhythms, she figured. And then she'd always wondered: Why even return the gun after the first attempt? Was it fear, optimism, or shame that drove him back to the store? Maybe the new one was shinier, or it held fewer memories of failure. Actually, she thought to herself, you would have to blame the equipment. How hard is it to shoot your face off? And then to take care of the rest of it? Idly, Lucia wondered what happened to the gun after he was gone. Every time she heard the booms from down the street she thought: *shotgun.*

There was no reason that he'd want to kill himself this time, as the pastor had counterintuitively intoned at the final service. He had, by the great and gracious grace of God himself, persisted through the first with half a face, and he had a job until he was fired from it after the break room incident, and it's true that his wife had left him, but she was no good, a tool, from the beginning, maybe the cause of all his misery, so it was like a blessing, or like the divorce had amounted to a cosmic wash.

God never wants your death, he said: what he wants is your devotion.
That's what the card had said that Lucia sent to his finally ex-wife who
was not technically an ex-, since they'd never gotten around to the divorce,
meaning that she inherited the unspent sum he had received after set-
tling his ridiculous lawsuit against the shotgun manufacturer, and this
seemed to Lucia sort of unfair whenever she thought about it, but much
of her life had turned out this way, so who was to say?

There! A light! It flickered and kept flickering. Something new was burning. It was moving, like a keg of powder on a skateboard rattling halfway down the street before it overturned and sat there on its side. Or
maybe something attached to a dog, or in a bottle, designed to save you
from the cold. It was hard to tell. She winced and waited for the boom.
When it came it silenced all of that. Off went the car alarms. Great, she
thought. This was her least favorite holiday after Thanksgiving.

Her daughter—Cherelle—had died. Slipped off a bridge was what the
police report had said. Slipped: maybe. Was she pushed? Did she jump?
Indeterminate, it read. It was a kindness to have left it so, perhaps. They
hadn't done much investigating. They had rounded up no suspects, had
no solid theory of the crime, because they thought of it as probably not
a crime at all, or not a solvable one. Here was what might had happened,
they said. It was cold. Sometimes they found a body down there. It was
a beautiful ravine. It was a long way down. From beneath you could see
and listen to the world above go by. Lucia had gone down there and stayed
down there, thinking.

The final disposition of her eternal soul was of course at stake, being
confirmed (though lapsed) Catholic (why she'd ever been attached to
religion Lucia had never understood: look what it did for her, she'd think
later), and Lucia wished to find her way across the border keeping the
living from the dead—if she could find a way to get past it and return,
she would, she would find out the truth from Cherelle. That border was
porous: this much she knew. But how to stretch across the gap she wasn't
sure. Wasn't sure, not yet.

She couldn't think, mostly on account of the douchebags, and she
hated not being able to think.

It felt good to call them douchebags, though this thought was inter-
rupted by a colossal boom, something really special, she concluded from
the cheers coming somewhere down the street. Having had enough,
Boyle, her bravest cat, flew by, scrabbling on the hardwood floors toward

the basement where the whole crew of beasts cleaned themselves, dismembered bugs, and plotted their revenge.

Maybe they had graduated to guns, she thought. Could they be? Maybe she should call the cops, she thought. The neighborhood had diversified, and some people had moved out to the suburb ring, as if that was any kind of solution. Had she ever been in love with flame like this, in love with the trajectory of bullet? It was in her family, surely. What was it with guns? With homemade bombs? With improvised explosives seen in movies and video games? You had to be careful with homemade bombs particularly, she knew. Just a touch of static could set one off if you didn't ground yourself.

Another firelight lit up the shapes of a couple of them, douchebags both, scurrying away from the dumpster and laughing. Everyone went batshit about this time of year, lighting wicks and fuses and firing up the whole neighborhood. Lucia was tempted to show them a real big bomb, the kind that would take out a garage or a whole house, something they'd miss when it was gone. But then: a short break. Hot air. Silence.

Then another bang, another douchebag, but this one was followed by a pause, like something else had happened, and then a shriek that sounded an awful lot like pain, Lucia thought. She could hear whooping that quickly ceased, incredulous, and then whimpering and a couple of voices, a wild moan that sounded like something never seen on earth, and, a couple of minutes later, banging on the door at the bottom of the street. Then nothing. A shout but not with words. Banging on the door next door, where the senile guy lives with his pickup truck completely filled with newspaper-dispensing boxes, clearly winched up from the ground, with bits of concrete and bolts trailing and shaking as the truck bounced by on its slow everyday patrol down to the VFW. Nothing at that door either. It was lightning moving quickly up her way.

She went downstairs. She was already feeling vindicated.

She opened up the door before the douchebag had had time to bang on it. That it was a crying boy she had not expected. She saw blood and a hand wadded up inside a T-shirt that advertised a band she didn't know.

It was obvious something had gone wrong between the douchebag and his fun and now she would be expected to help.

Of course his friends had gone.

She had him come in, got a bunch of ice and put it in one of her daughter's socks, which she still found strewn throughout the house in unlikely places, and that she had collected in the kitchen, her favorite

room, in a sort of laundry shrine, ever since her death. She told him just
hold this on it. Keep it compressed. It wasn't healthy to keep all the stuff,
she knew, or she was told from another show, but it was good she did,
she thought now, because she was prepared to help.

He blubbered but did what he was told. His face was a page of streaks
and ashes. Lucia asked him where he lived, if anyone else was home. No
such luck. She'd have to get him to the hospital herself. Or else watch
him continue to cry like this for hours, and bleed out. She weighed her
options.

She thought about herself weighing her options and weighed that as
an option. Sometimes when she thought about herself thinking she got
really recursive and would have to bottom out or go on, paused, nearly
forever. These times she forgot the right human interaction, and it often
came off as strange.

He moaned though, and it brought her back.

Are all the fingers there or do we have to find them? Give me a look,
she said.

They were there. They were mostly there. What was left of them was
still attached as far as she could tell, so she wouldn't have to take a
flashlight and ice-filled cooler out into the street. Was the kid looking at
her? Analyzing her inaction? Wondering about her own family with all the
deaths? The kid just looked at her. His eyes were zeros, giving nothing
back. It looked like shock to say the least. The clock was moving on the
wall. She clapped the fan system off and went for the door. At least she
wouldn't have to touch him, probably.

Waiting for him in the emergency room where it seemed like everyone
was covered in blood or had something protruding from their body—
that was some familiar fun. She hated being in the world like this, so
close to the bloody and dispirited, the deranged and lame. They were all
so fucking *present*, with their weeping and their remonstrations. They
took all your attention. That's why they had to wait in the waiting room.
They would not die, but their wounds looked so terrible that triage could
not come quickly enough. Of course she could handle it, but after her
house emptied itself out, she had thought she'd had the last of that.

Probable suicide daughter had at the least outlived her brother, who
had died in a car accident when he was fifteen, before he had any right
to be driving a car at all, and certainly before Lucia would have okayed
him getting his learner's permit, given his family history of recklessness.

He had stolen his friend's parents' car and flipped it on the interstate. You could consider that suicide, too, but the police did not, and spared her that. Maybe it was. It sure seemed that way to her. But the space between suicide and recklessness is occupied by teenagers, and was inaccessible once you left those years behind.

Almost as if to make exactly that point, Cherelle had gone a year later off a footbridge at the college she was attending, and Lucia wondered if Cherelle had waited out of spite or out of politeness, if she had waited for her mother to recover from the first loss before getting the second one underway?

Or was it really possible that she had slipped?

What did it feel like? It felt like Lucia was in a forest, as it went from twilight to black, so gradually that you couldn't even tell that you could no longer see your surroundings, and she found herself alone. Everything she saw seemed weakened after that: colors, light, the appealing precision of her instruments at the lab, sexual arousal, even the birds as they streaked south: there seemed to be fewer (and had she finished the survey she considered, she would have seen that she was in fact correct). She assured herself she noticed less, but as her world had changed, so did the one outside her windows.

It wasn't so terrible, though, after all, to have survived her children, she thought, in spite of the advice and knowing looks she had been given by people who meant well, who thought they knew what losing all your children meant because they'd read about it in a book that won a prize. You just go on. You get divorced if you weren't before. No one stays together, not really, after that. Even if one of you somehow made it back to hope, the other wouldn't, and would resent the one who'd found the path, and the marriage would burst from there. The only exceptions were those who believed in gods who mandated never splitting under any circumstances and whose authority bizarrely remained intact, even in spite of all the evidence to the contrary.

In a way it's freeing, Lucia said, eliciting shocked looks. She wondered if something had broken off in her. There's less to hold you here, to hold on to, less gravity and fewer dishes, she said. She made a chemistry simile that was not well recieved. You don't feel as bad closing your windows now. You stay in. There wasn't much out there left to see, honestly. Present company excepted, of course: you, my friends, remain important. (They did not.) She felt so unbound—light, really, she told herself; it was lightness she was feeling—she found it hard to believe that if she tipped a cup off the counter edge, it would fall and shatter. Later, her friends would explain Lucia's comments to their husbands and to each other as a response to shock, surely that was what it was.

Sometimes Lucia felt like she was going back in time, the years unwinding from a giant wooden spool, the kind on which power lines came wrapped, the kind you could flip up and use as a table if you were a kid.

Quite obviously Lucia was not much of a parent, or else her family got the wrong idea about the afterlife, or how bad their lives were, or possibly there was something in the blood or, more likely, in their brain chemistry. At one time she tried to track it down, tried to isolate the variables and assess the data. That both kids had died suggested correlation, if nothing more. And with them gone was she even a parent anymore? Could one have that title stripped for cheating or failure or whatever? Or was it a resting state you remained in for the rest of your existence? Instead she watched the neighborhood, tracked what she could, took copious notes. She had binders full of data: numbers of explosions per minute, per hour, per day; average rate of speed of cars; the incidence of revving sounds heard at night from a mile or two away as men raced in their souped-up Civics; instances of attempted and successful conversational interactions on the sidewalk, in the driveway, and at the entrance to her house. How many days it took the power company to rescue the tied-together pairs of shoes kids threw over power lines to signify whatever it was they were supposed to be signifying.

And, to be honest, if asked, Lucia would tell you that she herself had thought of suicide. Who wouldn't? Of course she had. She had thought it was the only way to know for sure. It became all she could think about sometimes. Her life was surrounded by it. Attenuated by it. She attended to it, and to the rigmarole that came along with it: support groups, stupid calls, being surrounded by bodies at the memorial service wanting to touch her except they wouldn't, most of them, because they were afraid her story might rub off on them, as if bad luck could be communicated by touch. She wondered sometimes: *Could* it? Certainly it gathered and it weighed. If she could disperse it like static electricity with a touch, should she, even if she could? It made no sense, of course: the world she had spent her life investigating did not work like that. But still the thought kept coming back in unguarded moments. Who could blame her if she had thought of suicide? Was it not her life? Couldn't that much of it drive someone to, well, anything? But Lucia would be damned, she said, if she would not persist until the world would yield or reveal its long-hidden heart. She clapped her hands and the clapper mechanism shut the air-conditioning off. This, she thought, was not something you just threw away.

The kid's name was Luis, he said. Or maybe Louis. He seemed ethnic, so she assumed. He sort of looked like a murderer—grim and bandaged, penitent, empty, stunned, as if he'd done something he'd have to answer for in the next life or when he got home. To him she looked like just another white disconnected lady neighbor, so they had this mutual opacity in common. Who knew anyone's story really?

His hand was saved, albeit with some tendon problems. He'd have a tough time with arthritis when he passed through middle age, a doctor said. Maybe don't take up the guitar or flute, he said, ha ha. You never know: maybe we'll make some advances between then and now, she said. The doctor looked at her, thought her optimistic, but didn't say so, his eyes narrowing. Calls had been made to Luis's parents, relieving her of responsibility, and it was only a matter of time until the sobbing mother came. She would emote enough for the both of them, for the whole moaning mass of the emergency room.

Luis was almost cute, she guessed, now that they got the blood cleaned off. They were cute when they were small and guilty, even as their hands could start something loud and amazing and do things to you that you never even dreamed they could—and when she went in to see him he looked up at her, his eyes streaky, painkiller-glazed. Lucia said she was going to go, that the nurses were going to take good care of him, that his mother was surely coming, but that she had very important things to do. She had a mind to go find his friends, waiting in their own homes for news of him by text or call, wondering what kind of stand-in for all of them he had become. Luis gaped at her, and his reaction time was slow, maybe because of the medication, and in that gap, she gave him a kiss on the forehead that would leave no lasting mark and disappeared back through the hallway, her heels clicking against the tiles.

People disappeared here all the time. You brought them into the emergency room and they would disappear behind the swinging doors into the muffled world. If their injuries were not immediate they would come back out to wait like everyone else under the softly humming lights.

Or if it was bad, they'd never make it back at all. At times Lucia had waited and waited, and the patient would not emerge. Her husband had disappeared here, and had not been able to come out unassisted. He had been up in his crane, towering three hundred feet above the worksite below, the set of massive holes they had blasted to make way for what everyone expected would become a new subterranean parking garage, and he had been hit by lightning in a storm. It had happened before: the cabin that controlled the crane was grounded after all, made storm-safe in theory, but something had gone wrong this time, and that was why, she'd tell herself later, she hadn't wanted him to take the job, or at the least, to come down when the weather turned south, like she had premonitions or something. He had told her he always did, though she found out later this was a lie. In fact, he never did. It took thirty minutes to get up or down, a three-hundred-foot climb on a semi-protected ladder in the middle of the scaffolding, and he would instead just wait it out each time with his stash of pornography that she knew he had—magazines or novels, sometimes ones with a semblance of a story, something to connect yourself to, and after the lightning strikes and the silence after, when he had been removed, the other workers had tried to keep this truth from her, a thing she was thankful for, and she was happy to let them divvy his stash up among themselves.

He would sit up there with his American Spirit Ultralights and his reading material (he had confessed to her once that it gave him a feeling of power, to masturbate that far above the ordinary workings of the ordinary people moving around the streets in grids, and what was she supposed to say to that?), and he would wait out the storm.

This time, others had seen lightning strike the tower, the highest point for a couple of miles, no less than a dozen times. One of his friends had told him later it was more like a hundred, but that seemed like the sort of lie that grows with each retelling, like the one about the kid they found in the forest when they were camping. She imagined it like a plasma globe, the kind you put your hands on and all those electric lashes licked you from the center, as if for once he was the center of the universe, everything striking around him, and how it must have felt to know whatever there was to know. And then there was a short or something, and he had been struck, and had radioed down using Morse, since his voice was gone, and it took them almost an hour to decode the static clicks. They had had to go up and bring him down, and they had called her, and she'd met them at the emergency room, which was when he went through those doors and returned somewhat less than he had been before. He was an invalid, and had to stay on the top floor of their house from that day forward until he died, eventual mercy for the both of them and for the kids, just a year later. Lucia had done everything for him, and it was hard on them both, but she had done it out of love, then anger, and then respect and a vague sense of obligation after those two things had burned away. And then he, too, had disappeared. Had taken his own life, in the way of her family. It was without her knowledge, but had she known, she would have approved. That's what she told herself later, and that's how the memory stayed with her—like a tiny pin, the kind you'd use to stick photographs or butterflies on corkboards or point out on a map where you came here from; except she had eaten it and it had stayed lodged within her for the duration of her life, or until her stomach acids would finally digest it or it would painfully pass through.

Maybe because of this instead of leaving, she waited another hour in the waiting room, and Lucia asked the nurse if the boy's parents had been contacted, and if someone was coming. Maybe she should have stayed with him in the room; she could have hummed or held his hand or told him dirty jokes. But then what had her parenting been worth, she wondered, and she knew that everyone else must suspect this failing in her, too, so she sat, fingers locked, out in the emergency room waiting room and watched a television show where police agents found The Lost (cue creepy humming sound). She had seen it before. It was all right—not that well written, but dark enough, because they didn't always find the missing one. About half the time they'd be alive. Some of the missing showed up dead. And a few were never found at all. Those numbers were way above the actual: no one would tune in to see one out of every eight (at best) found at all, in any way, alive or dead. No one wanted to see the ones who were gone completely, who had disappeared without a note or trail of leaking gasoline or fingerbone to signify their disappearance. And no one would tune in for the episodes where disappearances went completely unremarked, just a smoke sign left in the air, evaporating, like in cartoons.

Lucia watched the door open and close until a woman came in with the look: sufficiently desperate, sweaty, and uninjured. This would be Luis's mother, unaccompanied, her face pale, storming up to the reception desk to announce herself.

As she rose from the stained chair, Lucia realized the two of them had met. The mother might not remember her from that block party.

It would have been before Luis was born and they were both someone
other than who they had become. Lucia's husband was still alive then,
if flagging and in no shape to attend the party, which meant both the
kids were part of the equation. Since there were four of them still in the
house they went to parties, though the kids didn't come to the block
party for some reason, something stupid, probably, like they wouldn't
have mini corn dogs there, only regular corn dogs, and it might have been
when Cherelle was vegan. Where had they gone instead? They wouldn't
have stayed at home. Oh, the artificial lake: they must have been there
with their friends. Who knew what they did out there?

So Lucia had gone herself.

It was an unusually chaotic party, it being another Independence
Day with everyone trying to prove their patriotism, this being only a year
after those terrorist attacks down in Phoenix, you know the ones, the
ones that started all the fires, and for some reason now we kept blowing things up to show our resilience to our stuff getting blown up as if
to say *we*, not *you*, are the ones who blow stuff up: we do it for fun and
all the time.

Was fire fun then? There seemed to have been a lot of fires then.

And there had been two fires at the party, too, the first one due to
male-assisted lighter fluid overuse, and when it was put out all the sur-
rounding kids had cheered, then got bored, and muttered off, and the
dads held their heads low for a while but didn't apologize, or at least not
in public. Always awkward at parties, Lucia had rapidly gotten very drunk
and thought of her husband at home, above the street and looking out,
expecting her back any minute with a bratwurst for his consumption.

She did not, right then, want to go—not back to him, or anywhere else.

There was a second fire, too, wasn't there? Lucia had been talking to
Luis's mother about something trivial when the stop sign had erupted in
flames ten feet behind the two of them, and Lucia could only remember
a little bit of this: first the eyeshadow of Luis's mother, something bright,
an echo of the fire, and then a whoosh of air behind her, the illuminated
sign reflected in her glasses as she turned, elbowing someone else in the
back, and as she turned, the ghostly shriek of a child as if a poltergeist
had just caught fire and was surprised to find that it could burn.

The two women had ducked for cover, spilling their drinks onto
the street. They watched the colored alcohol trickle down toward the
sign and touch the burn but not, thankfully, catch flame. Luis's mother
crossed herself, and everyone else stood a little more alertly. The men

appeared immediately, clamoring to do something to demonstrate their worth, all yells and whooping, putting out the sign with tablecloths from the front yard. This was now and would be henceforth remembered as the Party of the Fires. Also the Last Party for a Couple of Years.

She remembered the mother from that party. How many years ago was that? Turning, the mother scanned the waiting room, looking for something or just bored, waiting to be ushered in to deliver love and reprobation to Luis. She was filled with purpose; she held it like a glow. Lucia could almost see it coming off of her, like holy flame.

Lucia stood. She should go to her, she thought, and did.

She was pleased with herself for taking this small action. She passed an adult covered in what looked like eighty staples in his arm.

As Lucia approached the mother, a nurse called another name, and the mother turned.

Lucia realized she had forgotten the woman's name, if she had ever known it. Had the world become so closed to her that it had become inaccessible?

The mother was just a foot away, preoccupied. Just beyond her the door led back into the real world.

Lucia reached out tentatively to touch the mother's shoulder. The mother turned again just before and the two bumped. Oh, I'm sorry, Lucia said.

It's okay, the mother said, her eyes already swimming away. They may have scanned Lucia's face, or maybe that was just Lucia wondering if she would be remembered. She wanted to say, Do you remember, you know, the fire? The party? That afternoon? How it felt to be who you were then? Can you still access it now? What would you give up for that knowledge?

Lucia's mouth stayed open for a beat. She could feel it gape. That pause went on just long enough to have contained some additional energy, but where it went was another question. Lucia couldn't say what, if anything, passed between the two of them.

Lucia closed her mouth. The mother's name was called, and she turned away and walked right through the gate into the hallway toward her son.

As for Lucia, she backed away. She went through the open door and disappeared.

It Is Hard Not to Love the Starvationist's Assistant

The job description was accurate: Assistant Needed for Commercial Body Modification Project. Sherilyn was excellent at assisting, having done it most of her life. She was certified to assist the nurses who would visit her grandparents in their home, where they would eventually die—together, in flames, probably though not conclusively one last act of rebellion against the world that had always, in their view, conspired against them. She had assisted dozens of her friends with their writing in college—plagiarism, really, though no one called it that then. Had driven getaway for her high school boyfriend's second vandalism spree (two hundred plus broken windows, flares shot up over the water like fireworks trailing into glitter, all the parking meters downtown winched up from the concrete then left there like used toothpicks for giants), and admittedly it was sort of under duress, if that's what you'd term their love, though she would have rolled on him in a minute if she had somehow been caught. Still, she could be counted on to show up on time, appropriately attired, prepared for almost anything, at any time, and to see whatever through. If she were a boy she would have been a Boy Scout, peppered with pins and multicolored badges, having mastered Webelos and on her way for sure to Eagle. Which is why she kept getting hired for these jobs. Her references: impeccable. Her work record: spotless. This was a kind of genius, she told herself, to be the supporting cast, even if you never got to call yourself a protagonist.

She had little respect for the body with its interlocking systems of fluids, its hormonal bursts and spurts. Where had it ever got her, she thought, and she was happy to help tame it when she could, she said at the interview. Her job was to be professional, to maintain lists, to watch the Subject's food intake, to monitor the Subject's weight as it slowly—then increasingly quickly, accelerating as the body began to burn its fat reserves—dropped, approaching the contractual goal. She would also be responsible for administering small electric shocks to curb undesired behavior, and occasionally for doing other things as needed. The need for discretion went without saying.

The Starvationist was a behaviorist at heart, with a bit of the dietitian's training and a strong streak of the dominatrix. Her fashion reflected this—chokers, leather strips, keychain handcuffs that her Assistant assumed must be a joke, and a complicated strappy mask she wore in all official Encounters with the Subjects. The look was a put-on mostly. She called it her game face, and it always struck Sherilyn as odd. When she asked, the Starvationist told her that it reassured the supplicants, I mean the Subjects. That's half of it, she said. They wanted to be reassured, to feel that by someone's holding them they could assert control. This is exactly what they lacked, and she gave it to them. So you had to look the part. You can detach, submerge into the role, and act. Sherilyn was asked to wear only red and black, something professional with a touch of sexy. She would be the carrot; the Starvationist was the stick. This was how it was explained to her. Nearly any human behavior could be curbed like this. Every other Friday she'd get to be the stick too.

Take this Subject, for instance: he could benefit from the stick. At forty-six, not an age past salvage but an age when the outlines of your life have long become clear: whatever the glass was, half-empty or half-full, the line was calcified on the side of the container. Sherilyn could tell he was a sort of sad guy, just out from what he'd termed an open marriage, the sort of open marriage that you sensed was more open on his side than on his wife's, that that was the story he'd been telling himself, that it was what she deserved for no longer wanting sex with him. He'd looked defeated, coming in, and was, no doubt. But he had one killer feature: a full head of hair, glossy and almost false looking, which he'd grown out to the point that it was hard to read it as anything but a performance. He had contracted the Starvationist to help him reach his weight-loss goal, which was to drop no fewer than sixty pounds. He wanted to get his old self back, he said, find his mojo. The usual. He wanted to impress girls. One in particular, he said: his ex. He wanted her back. He'd done something to lose her, though what that was he wouldn't say. Now he'd do anything. Become anyone. He'd tried a lot of things, he said, but none of them had worked. What did she want anyway, he asked Sherilyn, and she couldn't say of course (except for the obvious).

It could almost make you blind, encountering this kind of sadness
on the daily. You could see from the cabinets and garbage in his house
that this was a last chance for him. She saw it all on the walk-through
now, just Sherilyn and him, gathering data for the Starvationist.

He had all the products seen on television. A box of brochures and
glossy folders from weight-loss seminars. Hypnotism only works, Sherilyn
told him, for one of three people, those who are predisposed to those sorts
of states, and you are not. It's not your fault. Don't worry, she had said.
We'll get you there. You'll get to see the inside of that meditative state.
People often find that once they get beyond the first two stages of the
Process they begin to lose sight of their lives. They come out beautiful;
they come out changed.

Another Subject was this actor who needed to lose forty-one pounds
for what he clearly thought would be an Oscar-winning role. He was
supposed to be an ascetic, a sexy historical priest, and while the studio
told him they could digitally reduce him onscreen if they had to, he was
a method kind of guy, and needed to get there for real, to get inside
the body of a 110-pound man, for it to feel yes, the click, so right. He
had got down to 132 by himself through diet and exercise, deprivation.
He'd tried the Zone, low carb, all pineapple, et cetera, but he plateaued
at 132; 132 was skinny, but it was not 110. He was spinning his wheels,
he'd said when Sherilyn was doing the initial interview, and his people
couldn't get him down any further, and if he didn't he would lose the
role, and he would lose momentum, he'd said, whatever that meant, and
when Sherilyn had asked he'd said you know, the story, the one where
you are the next; when you lose that moment you're the previous, the
last; the roles stop coming. He said he had heard the Starvationist was
the breast. He actually said *breast*, and then corrected himself, laughing, and then Sherilyn laughed with him. She had liked his last movie,
though she didn't (would never—she didn't want to be one of the masses
who deify those whose lives occur onscreen) tell him this.

The job was mostly good. She got to talk to the famous, the semi-
famous, and the very very depressed because they were not more famous,
and that was a perk. It kept things in perspective. Here was what you
wanted, and here was what you had to do to get it. It was a simple story
that they told. Everyone seemed to feel the same: they wanted and they
wanted. Even those who'd appeared to be themselves, to be happy: inside
they wanted worse than anything. They just wouldn't—or couldn't—say.

The Starvationist held her at arm's length for a few months before she relaxed. She'd make a joke while prepping a Subject for anesthesia. And then she'd reveal some hidden section of herself in that beautiful moment when the Subject went under, like her interests in erotic asphyxiation or her now-decades-long fandom for the band Hanson (this was how Sherilyn learned that Hanson superfans called themselves fansons). Sherilyn had never watched someone die, but she wondered how much like death anesthesia was. It was breathtaking, like watching someone walk off a cliff. They made a joke, and then the self was gone. It would come back after the procedure, but where did it go when it wasn't here? Witnessing this *did* call for some kind of revelation, so Sherilyn began to tell stories too. And with every moment like this the two of them were stitched a little more closely together. The Starvationist said that she was glad she could rely on Sherilyn. She'd had trouble finding the right person. She gesticulated with the scalpel. Assistants wouldn't stay past the first three months. Why was what? she wondered. I've never quite understood. Then she addressed the unconscious Subject: Do you know? And when he did not answer back, she recollected herself and gestured back to Sherilyn: How about you? Why are you still here? I don't mean to seem ungrateful, but I'd resigned myself to replacing you like all the rest.

I couldn't say, Sherilyn said: I mean I don't know. I like the job. You help people.

We help people, Sherilyn.

I know, she said.

We change people, Sherilyn.

Yes, she said. It's hard to change, to really change.

Yes.

Sherilyn saw the bodies melt away, the sags and flaps develop, because that was what happened when you lost a lot of weight in a very short time. Sometimes that spare footage rubbed together and you had to grease the rubbing parts if you run, which almost no one ever did. It wasn't always pretty, this kind of care. Keep your clothes on, Subjects were told, until you see the cosmetic surgeon, if that matters to you.

The system works in part on fear and bargaining. The testimonials on the brochure explained that one former Subject was able to leach the last twenty pounds into the middle toe of his right foot, and then they lopped it off. He lost the toe but he did make his weight. The guy was really, truly happy to be down to what he weighed when he graduated from high school and got the first of his four lifetime Camaros. The middle toe doesn't do jack for you, he said—who thinks about that toe?

It doesn't help with balance, doesn't make you faster, more beautiful, cooler, or otherwise better equipped for life. He was thin now and life could not be better, he said. He beamed. The camera loved him and always would. Sherilyn had her doubts. He went on too long, especially for a testimonial. They couldn't identify him by name, but they mentioned a couple of movies he had been in before the treatment and the blockbuster that came after. Still. Sherilyn wondered: What would have really happened if he hadn't made the weight?

Almost no one doesn't make the weight, the Starvationist said.

But what if?

He would have lost something bigger, the Starvationist said.

For instance: the whole amputation thing was real and written into the contract. She didn't doubt whether it happened—she had seen the toe stump, had helped pull it off and preserve it in ice, so she knew it did—but it seemed awfully grisly. The Starvationist had a cat named Spragmos, which was something unattractive from some ancient Greek myth. The cat was ugly, bloated, angry, fat, not sleek and clean like other cats. He had a big hump along its back. Was missing a tooth in the front so he often appeared to snarl even when he was apparently pacified. He bit you in the head while you were sleeping, she explained. Sherilyn wondered why you'd even have a cat like that. Love, the Starvationist had said. He hadn't always been this way. When you have a pet, you commit.

So commit her Assistant did. The job became all-encompassing. It was all she thought about, even at home or walking through the city, waiting for something to happen to her. When she began to dream about amputation Sherilyn knew she had become part of something true. So when Paul, an ex-boyfriend, walked in for an afternoon appointment, she felt almost—what—violated, she thought, later, once she'd recovered from the shock. And god, what had become of him? She'd heard from mutual friends that Paul had changed in the wake of their breakup. He had grown quite large indeed (the gossip suggested it was grief and desolation over losing hold of her heart, her heat, her gleaming, perfect teeth—that her spurning broke a boundary inside him, and he just inflated).

Or it might be just that his name contained his destiny. That was his theory. He'd always hated it, being one of the Pauls, but being in a relationship had protected him from it, himself, his doom, he'd said.

Name one successful Paul, he'd said, when they had been dating for a year.

McCartney, Sherilyn replied.

Second fiddle, but alive and married to a woman with just one leg, he said: so there's that. But okay, name another.

She got distracted: there's *what*? He was alive and married, a multi-millionaire. She paused before responding. How about the apostle?

Is that successful?

He's remembered, right?

Wasn't he crucified or pulled apart by dogs or something awful?

He might have had a point, though, when she thought about it, and she spent a whole weekend trying to disprove his theory, and this was the conversation from the relationship that came back to her from time to time, and she'd never had a great answer, which was pretty strange, you had to admit, because how much could a name really determine? (Don't ask a John.) Eventually the best she figured out was: Bunyan, some baseball player for Milwaukee famous for a string of hits in consecutive games, and probably some pope somewhere along the line (John Pauls do not count, he reminded her). Paul Simon?

Among the more transcendent of the natural Pauls, but we only remember his name in contrast to the dorkiest-named partner you could dream up.

Shit. How about J Paul Hurhston, the famous horror writer?

J, my dear, is for John.

Hmm, she said.

Compare the success of Pauls, he said, to Johns. I give up, she said, and did.

It had been a year.

Paul had contacted the Starvationist, though he had first referred to her as the Interventionist, mixing her up with one of those jokers who specialized in curbing any old kind of behavior unwanted by families on television shows. When he had called, his voice was unrecognizable—thick and thinky, like he had spent far too much time alone, in his head. Who knows how many loser Pauls he'd now collected? It's like his vocal cords had gotten fat, too, if that was even possible. Luckily, maybe, he didn't recognize Sherilyn either, until he had come in for the initial consultation, which was a little more than awkward, and the Starvationist could surely sense it. If he wasn't sure when he'd walked in, the look on Sherilyn's face—impossible to hide—was what clicked for him, he said, later: that was what now committed him to the Method, the full course of it.

She explained their history to the Starvationist.

Good, she said. Stakes are important.

Sherilyn was not so sure. Shouldn't you be here on your own? she asked. People will do a lot of stupid things to try to get back someone who it turns out they cannot have.

He'd explained that his weight had increased ever since she left, it was all he could think about, eating, the slow roll down the inclined plane of their love (he was an engineer and worked hard for these kinds of metaphors). Was there a maximum blood pressure you could get to and still be alive?

Lord, he said, give some salt to Paul.

Now he—and via the magic of institutionality he became Subject, no longer Paul or he at all—looked like a sandwich, his brow inflated, his neck inflated, the totality of him mushrooming outward, and it was all Sherilyn could do not to let her horror out. She had heard, of course, what everyone had said, but she doesn't believe in talking to one's exes. And especially in this case, she had thought it better just to cut it off entirely—you don't want to leave men with hope.

As part of the Contract Meeting, Paul was informed that it was a possibility—possible, though rare—that he might have to lose an extremity as part of the treatment, but that he got to pick which one, if it came to that, and he had to pick now, so there would be Actualization of Consequence.

Of course he had to pick the penis.

Almost no one picked the penis. Though one man picked his lover's penis, and then became petulant when informed the extremity had to be his own. After that he—like most people—picked a toe, though it didn't end up needing to be clipped off.

Toes were the easiest, the least obtrusive, amputations. Very few people had any love for the toe, aside from the array of sandal sniffers, stocking stuffers, and foot fetishists who inevitably found their way to the Starvationist, fetishists drawn inexorably to another, usually through the power of the internet. Occasionally you got the people who wanted amputations, who were that particular brand of fucked up, the Starvationist told Sherilyn. That's why they did the psych screen up front, the MMPI, those weird Rorschach cards, and the rest of the battery of tests. That way you could control certain variables, keep the real wackos out, those who didn't *want* to succeed, for whom the consequences *were* the endgame.

Runners never picked the toe, but runners never came to the Starvationist, having already found their system.

Afterward Sherilyn told the Starvationist that he probably wouldn't do it, if it came to it, that he'd pick another body part. Who would really want it to be the penis? she said. You never know, the Starvationist told her in another one of those unguarded moments that became almost startling: her father had chemically castrated himself to reduce the incidence of one of his many compulsive urges.

But that's different, Sherilyn said, he still had the body part, right?

That's true, said the Starvationist.

Sherilyn asked, Is he still alive?

Yes, she said. Kind of, she said. I don't want to talk anymore about it. Well, with this Subject we will see.

What kind of life would it be with the sex drive just stripped from you—or would it remain a learned compulsion? It must have been pretty bad, she thought. But then a lot of it was pretty bad, she found, working here.

And besides, Paul's penis, like most penises, was never one of his better features, though perhaps now with his massive weight gain its position had improved, thought Sherilyn. Maybe it too would become weighty when engorged, would sway from side to side like a pendulum. This was not a thought she had ever thought before, she realized, with some alarm, and wondered where it came from.

The Method is rough, what with the collars and the tourniquets, the tubes, and the restricted diet, but the worst part for Subjects was the lack of sleep. There were no drugs. The Starvationist did not believe in drugs, believed instead in the power of the will, and of suggestion, and of threat and consequence. Her father's chemical castration didn't take, she said, later, in another unguarded moment. He had done some things, and it was ordered by a judge; this was another era, when that still happened, but it didn't help. They had found out later that he'd taken reverse hormone therapy to bring back his sex drive: he said he just couldn't live without it. And he had committed another crime, and had to be removed to an experimental camp, and he had returned completely changed.

Changed how?

Just changed. He wasn't the same. Less there, really, which honestly was better. He could be a terror before. Now he was just a shell of one.

Her Assistant wondered: Was that where it began for her?

The Subjects were nearly all able to make their goal weights. They lost tens of thousands of pounds in the aggregate. There was Danny, a four-hundred-pounder who lost, with their help, half of his body size in just under a year, though he died shortly afterward from an unrelated

condition that no one was aware of. His testimonial still appeared on
the brochure, with the before-and-after photos, accompanied by an asterisk and type so small it was illegible except with a magnifying glass.
It had to be specially printed on a super-high-resolution printer: There
Are Health Reasons Not to Suddenly Lose All Your Body Weight. And
Sherilyn was impressed and a little bit surprised when each of them
finally made their weight, in spite of what she knew about the Method,
which worked whether or not you wanted it to. That was its genius. That
was why the Starvationist could charge such fees, why she could afford
to pay an assistant as extravagantly as she did. When everything else
has failed, you should call the Starvationist. That was the little jingle the
ad agency had created, which Sherilyn found herself humming. Sherilyn
didn't know why they'd bothered with advertising, since almost all their
business aside from the internet wackos came from word of mouth.
There is no shortage of those hoping to lose (or even occasionally gain:
the Starvationist did this too) weight in this world, and they all come eventually to the Starvationist. Working here Sherilyn had started to notice
how omnipresent weight was, how advertisements gestured toward its
loss everywhere and in every medium: television, newspapers, internet,
magazines, even stapled up on telephone poles all throughout the city
or plastered on the crowded, aging bulletin boards at the public library
and the coffee shop. Besides sex, this was now the great draw. There is
money to be made, people to be saved from themselves, from the imminent world.

At the end of the world there will be cockroaches, a few stalwart
lovers reaching out toward each other, some battlements, a shitload of
Styrofoam, weirdo constantly mutating viruses attacking each other or the
few remaining human hosts, and the Starvationist. That's what Sherilyn
told her friends who wanted to know why she stayed on. They asked:
Wasn't it just awful being around so much want? Wasn't it like a cult? And
could you tell us more about its dictates? About how it operates?

No. She stayed, she thought, because the Method worked every time,
unlike love, family, or autoerotic asphyxiation. Sherilyn saw it work: she
helped it work. She affixed the tubes, held the Subjects down, administered pulses of electroshock to the points circled into constellations on
their sometimes-willing skin. She drew the cutting lines and helped guide
the Starvationist's hands in the cases where it came to that. This was the
one task for which the Starvationist truly needed an assistant: her hands
got shaky when touching skin, when cutting. She had tried med school

before washing out of surgery. She just had a mental block, and could not get past it. This was her secret. And when Sherilyn started paying attention, she realized that the Starvationist never actually touched a Subject flesh to flesh. Not once. Hence the gloves and the getups and the masks. Here was what she was really needed for: the cutting and the touching. So Sherilyn would cup her hands on the Starvationist's until they stopped their little shaking, and—like Ouija!—would guide them sort of semimystically to do what they had to do. Once when the Starvationist couldn't do it, Sherilyn had to make the cuts herself unguided, which was far harder than she would have guessed: flesh unzipped so easily under the Starvationist's hands on her hands, and even though it seemed that Sherilyn did all of the work, alone, suddenly she was in her head with all those Pauls, and she nearly botched the cuts. The incision along the socket where the ring finger would have gone into was jagged, and needed another round of trimming or it might go septic. This particular Subject wanted the ring finger gone if something had to go. She had been deserted by her husband, who, after upending her from her friends and life in Minnesota, moved her to Tucson, Arizona, where after just six months, he confessed that he was gay and wanted a divorce. She asked: Why did he even want to move us here? Not *us* but *me*: he moved *me* here—and not even to Tucson proper, I don't know if you know it (it's a dusty little town) but even worse, to Rita Ranch, a shitty commuter suburb for those who worked down at the avionics corporation where they designed missiles or software for them or parts to help them fly straight and long and kill, and then he left me there. All the restaurants they went to there were chains. It burned her skin to go outside. Every plant had hooks or barbs, and sometimes you wouldn't even notice you got a spine in you until you went to bed. Some spines got so deep in you they wouldn't ever come out, not ever, she explained. And then with his boyfriend he moved right back to Minnesota and I was there alone in all that desert suburban fucking air.

So with this intervention from the Starvationist, she said, she would finally be done with all of it. Had she even *tried* to lose the weight? Who cares? she said. It would be a fitting reminder of what was there and would never return, even as she could now fit back into a size ten, something the husband had said she would never do again, and he didn't know what she could or couldn't do anymore, not now. And of course he came crawling back to her for support when his boyfriend left him in frozen Minnesota. You're my best friend, he'd said. You're the only one who really knows me. Back in a size ten, with her finger gone, she lost his name and switched her hair and returned to Minnesota. Her life would be hers again. Never again would she answer or return his call. You had to admire a woman like that for doing what she did, for recovering from that kind of wreck.

Was that the kind of wreck Paul was? He sure seemed wrecked, but Sherilyn could not see how it was her problem or her fault. He did genuinely seem to want change. It was uncomfortable being so close to him as he fell apart, even now that she was part of the solution.

The second time Paul saw Sherilyn in the office she could see him stiffen up, and not in the way she briefly used to love. He stammered for a minute, then got control, found civility, said hello. It's not like he didn't know she was here, that she was the hands around the Starvationist's hands, that she was part of what was happening to him now. So today, as usual, even when he wasn't late, Sherilyn told him he was early so he'd have to wait. That it could be some time. Expectation was part of the Method. Plus the Starvationist was with another Subject, an actor better known for his many nonacting passions that seemed like they must amount to either a mania or a joke. Normally she wouldn't say anything this specific, but she was put off by Paul and the beach ball of his engorged body, then the thought of possibly bearing some responsibility for it, and for his eventual future depenising if the Method didn't work, so she was off guard and stumbling. They both were. It was like their first date, which also went badly, involving diarrhea, a word he was completely unable to spell in the apology note he sent her, attempting to overcome her food poisoning and his botched attempt at cooking Thai. Back then Paul was beautiful, and his big skill, the thing he had mastered, was the ability to listen to Sherilyn as she told him about herself. He was all ear, all hammer and anvil and Eustachian tube and drum, and she had loved that immediately about him, this self-effacingness. He looked sort of dumb, too, and that was a plus.

The downside of this was that their relationship quickly became all about her, him hanging on her, always listening. She revealed herself to him, and got little back, until the great Pauling happened. It wasn't domination, nothing like that, but there was nothing to it finally—he could not emerge from this stance and tell her anything she needed—and so she soured even as he took more of her inside himself. In retrospect their vectors were diverging even after their first night together, and she assumed he was too dumb or proud to tell.

The actor, whom they both recognized, came out of the closed door and walked down the hallway, beaming in the way that actors do when they know they are recognized, when they do their public masking thing. Sherilyn and Paul locked eyes—he knew she would not dignify the actor with her praise, and he was right. The actor passed between the two of them without comment. She wondered if the actor would feel let down, what that would feel like for him. He was looking thinner already, she thought, but didn't say.

Weeks passed.

Then more weeks.

And then just one more.

As the Method worked on the expanded version of Paul, the Starvationist's Assistant watched him whittle himself away. His behaviors normalized, then simplified, then some of them disappeared altogether. He took on this habit at times of seeming not to breathe, and Sherilyn wondered if it was real or illusion, if it was a literary allusion to some story by Kafka, Hurhston, or King, or Borges (his favorite authors, none of them, of course, an unadorned Paul), if he had some store of oxygen inside his sloppy body or if it was all a trick. He did it constantly, annoyingly, as Sherilyn charted his progress, the pounds slipping away, though the Starvationist was not concerned: she said this was not what was important. What was, Sherilyn wondered, and neither Paul nor Sherilyn asked themselves why she had given up on him and the Love That Was (grandiosely, he had referred to this in most of the dozen emails they had traded around the end of their relationship, recapping it in hopes of finding an alternate ending to their narrative), which she was thankful for. She did not want to talk about it here or elsewhere either, and because the Method depended on Excising the Personal (and possibly the penis), she had to quash it the one time he had tried to bring it up. He had to wear the Choker Apparatus for a day when the Starvationist noted this. It was a spike on his otherwise unremarkable chart, and after that his behavior curve improved, smoothed out. He was in the groove, right on trend, approaching norm. And as he was Reduced, he said less and less, and that was more as Sherilyn remembered him.

Then he plateaued for a week, and his chart went horizontal, requiring the Starvationist and her Assistant's intervention. She asked him: What was wrong? What had changed? Sherilyn was not supposed to do this; Subjects were tracked and redirected but not interrogated, but she couldn't help herself. She knew this was where the Possibility of

Amputation was turned into an Actual Scenario. They had to bring it out to be Examined, Photographed, and Considered, and if it was a humiliation, so much the better. The Subject gave in to tears, not for the first time, though this did not sway the Starvationist. It was either the last ten pounds—just ten pounds after all that work!—or he would lose the thing. Predictably Paul tried to back out, said he was happy the way he was, having lost a lot of weight already, nearly ninety pounds: that was a lot, he said, don't you think?

It was, but the contract had another number. The Method required, as Sherilyn explained and had explained before, the Full Weight Loss. It's guaranteed. We can do it the hard way or the hard way, she said.

She asked him: Why is it so hard for you to see this one thing through? (She wanted to ask him instead: Which one of us is the wreck you're diving in?)

He said: Why is it for you?

It was, wasn't it, Sherilyn thought, at least a little bit.

Why didn't he choose a different body part, she wondered, but couldn't ask because of the answer she feared he'd give. The air between them got weird.

Things the Starvationist doesn't know about Sherilyn, in spite of the rigorous examination she was subjected to in the job application process: she was once a large girl—at twelve, Sherilyn weighed 166, and her mother thought she might never stop expanding, since the kid was voracious, would eat almost anything. Her parents were vegetarians, but Sherilyn had discovered meat—bacon in particular—on sleepovers and visits to restaurants. They thought maybe Sherilyn's increase in mass was a genetic anomaly or some kind of hormonal imbalance: she sure was a hungry girl, didn't seem to be depressed or bulimic, acting out or wearing goth clothes or ostentatious thongs. Everything in the family was done by consensus, through logically argued points. Sherilyn took responsibility for her own upbringing, and she too agreed that she was getting further away from thin, from their family ideal. She assisted in the presentation about her deviation from the norm. Her parents were slim, worked out constantly, watched what they ate. It was oppressive; it was reassuring. It made her hungry.

Also: she was a lonely girl. This was less important to the future job, and was perhaps related to her weight, the swelling of her hands, the rapidly decreasing likelihood of anyone wanting to hold them tenderly at horror movies or out by the lake. But how do you measure loneliness?

Can you index it? Does it show up on tests? The answer was not really, not that it should matter anyway.

Suddenly, like a storm, her weight peaked, began to wane and melt away, for no good reason. No behavior change; no moral lesson. She ate the same, but her metabolism sped up, and by fifteen she was well beneath the state's cutoff line for obesity, which was admittedly pretty high. She was part of the solution, not part of the problem, and she would remember this. As she lost the weight, she felt more like she was becoming someone else, another self, a more attractive twin. And she was no less lonely, even as she started to acquire her first few variously criminal boyfriends whom she could then assist in their endeavors, who could take her from the life she led to another, more interesting one.

She had always wished, though, that she could have done it by herself, through self-control, through force of will, because this made her lazy, she always thought, or it introduced an uncomfortably irreducible mystery at the heart of the self. Maybe that's why she couldn't let it go. When she took on a new behavior, she couldn't change it easily. Couldn't change her mind. The obsessive rubbing at her skin, the self-administered burns, the occasional cutting, these were things she couldn't do anything about except to keep them covered up, to keep them secret, to keep them safe, her own. If the Subjects or the Starvationist saw this evidence, she wouldn't be kept on, she knew, and Paul knew these secrets, good as he was at letting her reveal herself. Appearance is important for the Method, for the Methodist church she used to attend before giving it up after her confirmation that confirmed church as a choice, a choice she now made to sleep in Sunday mornings and watch taped reruns of forensic television shows in which mysteries seemed to be solved, not deepened.

Two days closer to the deadline, things had not improved with Paul. He hadn't lost one more pound since last check-in, couldn't quite make it past plateau. The three of them sat down and consulted the photographs, the documentary evidence, the binding pledge, the signatures on all the paperwork. He presented some serious-looking language from his lawyer that the Starvationist just brushed away. It was all in order, simple, fixed: he would do it or he would not. He had less than a week now to lose those last ten pounds or they'd have to do their trimming thing. This happened in maybe five percent of the cases they took on. They would have to draw the weight into the appendage with the Apparatus and take it off. The success rate was important, inevitable. Ax that: it was essential.

The Starvationist's face—the part you could later see through the mask at the lopping ceremony—was beautiful and stern when she delivered the Ultimatum. She had this ability to completely drain herself of the human, to be assured, to be simple. It was more than an act—it was a talent. It was impressive. It made her like a machine, impenetrable like a battlement. Sherilyn admired her, or it might even have been love, she sensed, at times like these.

When the Starvationist was out of the room, she hissed at him: Just lose the fucking pounds. You're embarrassing. She will do it: she'll cut it off, take it away. This isn't a joke, she said. You need to do this for me, she said, and for yourself.

He moaned and mooned a bit, a trait Sherilyn always hated in retrospect, this way he could make himself seem guileless and faultless—she told herself it had always been like this, that she hadn't loved it for a while. It was clear he didn't believe that the two of them would do it, would amputate. He said, It's my party. I'll cry; I want to. He asked: And what if I ran? Would you come with me?

Paul, it doesn't fucking *matter*, she hissed. You will achieve your goals! And as if to demonstrate this, she fitted two straps around him and locked them down. This is to remind you of the pressure, she told him. It is what we do.

It's what *she* does, he said. You're just the assistant.

He was already forgiving her.

She put on another strap and jerked it tight. He could barely walk like this. This will release tonight, she said, automatically. You have three days, she said, and left him in his apartment with all the Star Wars posters on the wall. At least he finally got them framed. That was a kind of progress.

Later that night she could hear his moaning in her dream.

He wouldn't make the weight. He missed it by a pound.

It was only one pound, almost within the range of scale error! she was telling the Starvationist, her exclamation point nearly a plea (and she never pled on anyone's behalf, so what must she have thought of this?), but midsentence Sherilyn looked at Paul and in his eyes she saw, again, forgiveness, and so she hardened, too, and ceased her plea. Let that which Paul deserveth come to Paul, she thought.

The machine was spinning up. She could hear it hiss and spit.

The subject was on the table now, strapped in for the procedure. The chamber was rising, and with it they would bring the last pound out. The three of them would watch his penis swell, like in those ads you'd see in adult magazines, in the days before internet porn, for penis pumps, buff guys with ripped abs, their dicks in pumps getting jacked up like Christmas inflatables. Sherilyn had never understood that either: Did it feel good to see your dick that big? How long did it last before it shrunk? Paul was moaning now in anticipation, or maybe it was capitulation. Only he could know right now how it felt: Was it like freedom or something else? His eyes were closed, his mouth an O and then a line. The surgical tools gleamed on the disinfected felt.

The Starvationist and her Assistant locked eyes and hands. She placed her hands in Sherilyn's. What they had to do was done in a minute, pressure applied and bleeding stopped, the sentence ending not with a bang but with a mute hiss, the vacuum's release, an ellipsis attenuating itself finally to a period and then a blank. They had to wait for two minutes while the machine spun down. When Sherilyn had released the Starvationist's hands, she could feel something had changed. But what? She blinked up at the recessed lights. Now he would sleep for a day and he would wake under different lights, a new man, as they had agreed.

The light left streaks along her vision when she closed her eyes that would follow her for an hour, maybe longer. It was done. The weight was gone. The story would go out and be repeated, comma after comma after comma: anything about someone's dick seemed to go viral fast. And this one had all the elements people liked: a love gone bad, a redemption chance, a second act, an amputation scene, a metaphor. It would be something to be believed, or at least propagated. She didn't care whether it would be repeated. She wouldn't tell, herself. Was it even true? No matter. The Starvationist's Assistant would never leave, be able to doubt her job again, after this.

Everyone Looks Better When They're under Arrest

Once again, as we always do on weekdays now, after the nearly successful kitchen makeover soon to be featured on a television station near you through all the lines and waves propagated by satellites and repeaters somewhere (I can't tell you which station it will be on just yet—there are clauses in the contract that prohibit us from revealing this information, clauses that bind us to one action or to another, clauses that guide our responses to this thing we have chosen to submit ourselves to—I hold these clauses to me like I do paper money when it is warm and freshly pressed and I get lucky with it at the bank), we find ourselves waiting for the stove.

The stove never comes on weekends—or so we thought initially. The waiting is a saga that we repeat. We wake just after six because the contract stipulates that if the stove is to arrive that day, we will receive a call between seven and nine—this is before my wife's traditional time to wake, since she works late into the night and likes to sleep until ten if she can, which is not often anymore. If we are not there to receive the call, they will not attempt to deliver the stove, and the whole thing will repeat.

I imagine it as beautiful, no less an object of desire than the new BMWs both of my philandering brothers yearly covet. I think of them—brothers and cars and my future stove—on TV, in light, rotating on pedestals forever. I think of them as permanently under glass, on display. Wherever the stove is now, it is beautiful, I know, and it will satisfy us totally when it finally is installed.

Other things stipulated in the contract: that we will not reveal any details beforehand (thus that I am telling you at all may violate this clause—though this missive is only to be released upon our untimely deaths, or after the stove has arrived and the show has finally aired); that we cannot interfere in the actual filming of the episode; and that we will not benefit otherwise from the work. *Otherwise* means we cannot sell our story to the tabloids, or go on talk shows, or sue anyone in any way for any reason ever in this matter. If the show is killed for whatever reason—scheduling change, sweeps month, sudden cancellation, finding damning photographs of me, a surplus of photogenic pets, if the networks find a more entertaining and American couple—then at that point we are released from the contract, and as such are free to talk about the thing again. We will be unbound, like molecules of gas.

Our cat had to be kept off the new tiled kitchen floor, they said. It—persisting in referring to our cat as it, not she—was far too fat for television. (Have you watched daytime TV, I asked?) If it wanders into the scene, we'll have to scrap the shot, they said. What if she lost a lot of weight? we asked. They smirked and said nothing after that.

The contract specifies that the stove should have been in the warehouse and thus delivered to our house more than a month ago, barring unforeseen actions and consequences of cross-country shipping and publicity considerations from our sponsors, of which there are many and they are glorious, boasting warehouses full of gleaming surpluses and fat television budgets. It has not yet arrived, and the kitchen is bare—a desert, wide and luminous—without it. We have blinding white everything—new side-by-side fridge with deluxe ice maker (settings for cubed, crushed, chopped, and an unofficial setting for dented, nearly crushed, and spat out with great force so as to nearly crack our glasses); excellent new dishwasher; range hood above the space where the stove will be, lit by a superpowerful ultrafluorescent bulb in the shape of a halo; exhaust fan leading out through twenty feet of ductwork into the cold world outdoors; garbage disposal powerful enough to crush a jar of quartz (I've looked underneath the sink at the thing—it's as big as the propane tank); and a trash compactor designed to keep possible babies' hands out of it while it compresses. This kitchen of ours is a vision of potential heaven, if heaven was a domestic diorama.

Can we have sex in it? we asked, feeling that we needed their permission, or that we would enjoy the asking. We like anywhere that's new. Which might have been the wrong thing to say. The producer looked confused and left.

Another one will come along eventually.

All that technology waiting here for us, for you, and yet there is no stove.

Instead, there is a gas line poking up like a crocus from the glistening new tile.

Things that Jennifer, who is my wife (have I told you her name before? if not, this is an oversight, and I apologize; she chides me sometimes for forgetting to introduce her), thinks the lonely gas line looks like: a road winding up a mountain; a falling streamer swirling to the floor, caught midfall on camera; something from last year's Macy's Thanksgiving Day Parade (one of the floats, I think); a twist of bent-up DNA; abstract art; a toy for a giant metal animal; a hand thrusting up from the grave like the beginning of a zombie movie; the Statue of Liberty at the end of *Planet of the Apes*; a wick; an ashy firework worm; a snake.

One of our neighbors is a killer in the making, we are almost sure—if not the woman, then the man (either one will do). They are all broken glass and fist and fire. If all it takes is the right frame of mind and the right events—both motive and opportunity—the two of them are running for it, some front-page splash, some new great moment meant eventually for reruns of *CSI: Detroit*. Will we be upstaged by them gone combustible?

Jennifer is keeping tabs on this developing situation, as they refer to these kinds of things on the TV news. She says: I will keep you posted as the situation develops.

Their fate is, I think, closely tied to ours. This by virtue of proximity, by virtue of voyeuristic thrill and responsibility.

In the meantime we are stoveless, waiting, forced to get fast food, to go to Wendy's to get our meals biggie-sized. This is not product placement: we do like to go to Wendy's even after the demise of the Freshtastic food bar, so popular fifteen years ago, gone for health reasons, we presume. We love to be anonymous among the crowd, pending our new fame when it finally comes and the joy of not being able to leave the house for fear of paparazzi. Or: we ask our friends to have us over, over and over. Or: we microwave. I have a book, *Kids Cook Microwave*, from when I was young. This explains how to make many simple things, like eggs. Helpful tip: make sure you pierce the yolk to keep it from exploding.

The kitchen is made up to look like a fifties diner. We have been looking desperately through stores that sell actual memorabilia or sometimes even reproduction memorabilia (like the kind you see at Applebee's) for an old chrome toaster. And some other things that I just do not remember—I am the idea man; Jennifer handles the specifics. Hence whereas the diner theme is me, the exact reproduction tile is Jennifer (not Jen, not Jenn, not

Jenny or whatever, she will tell you: this is the first rule of dating, courting, or later being married to a girl named Jennifer—know which variation she prefers; in the Midwest there are so many of them, but my wife is Jennifer, not some terse and shortened version).

The kitchen stylists worked with us extensively to find just the right pieces to make the whole thing come together. To make it pop, they said. Their sponsors would provide us with the finest, newest appliances we could ask for: prototype models, one-of-a-kind advances in freezing technology seen only in demonstrations or glossy productions at trade shows then later reproduced in magazine spreads. Our freezer, it is true, can freeze almost anything about twice as quickly as any other consumer freezing appliance. We are assured of this. How about a food dehydrator, like I used to see on TV? I asked. They said sure, as long as it's approved by Jennifer in writing. I popped the question on her late at night just after sex, and she said yes—this came out in a rush—and this is good because I have loved them since when I was young. You remember the commercials—dehydrate your beef down into jerky! Any meat can be preserved without chemicals for years! Call the 800 number on your screen to try one for yourself. I did—though I was too young for credit cards, and thus legitimacy, I asked them a lot of questions about the thing, like, for instance, could it dehydrate flesh, as in human skin? The salesgirl had me talk to the manager, who, after thinking about it, said it would, in theory. They took my name and number. Nothing ever came of that. Jennifer says I am probably on some list of creeps somewhere.

I don't tell the producers that I dream sometimes of blood smeared across our new counters. I dream sometimes of stain, then static, and then other things. I think of women and a hundred inches of forgiving snow.

Why were we picked for this? we wonder. We entered no contests. Our kitchen was previously unremarkable (and thus a good candidate), but we lacked the emotional draw of most of those you see on TV—we are not orphans, ragamuffins who have just lost their parents to two simultaneous car crashes in different states the same year that their father was elected to the governorship of our fine midwestern state. We went to college. We have an okay life. One car. We're mostly white. Religious enough to pass. Middle-of-the-road. Old house with a cracking Michigan basement (this is the technical term for it, a sort of basement like a huge and sloping grave nearly impervious to erosion and water seepage, or so I theorize). Perhaps we represent a big segment of the viewing audience (meaning you, who are in most important ways like me; that is, at least

as most people are like one another; that is, as I believe in my better
moments). I have my theories about surveillance and our kitchen. Tiny
cameras. Voyeurism and webcasts. Teens on camera waiting just for you:
no credit card required. Someone somewhere is watching what we cook,
what we eat. Technically this could be you. We could be on TV even after
the camera crews have rolled their machinery back into the trucks and
left their ruts all around our lawn (they also put in new sod so our old
lawn would be again like new, and then of course they parked all over
it once they'd got the outside shots they needed). We could be the next
unwitting reality TV sensation—one giant psych-out at our expense.

Maybe there is something missing in our lives. I mean, beyond the
obvious.

Our sex life founders a little as we wait for the stove. They said last night
it had arrived at the warehouse—carted in by truck across the Plains
from its birthplace somewhere in Colorado, land of high-altitude special
cooking instructions and the Denver Broncos. My wife is asleep as I tell
you this—this night I am on watch for the thing; she will take the early
morning hours. But the one they sent was dented. Banged up. Dinged in
a minor way according to the voice that came across the phone to me
and was sometimes garbled or nearly dropped due to the spotty cellular
connection. And this was important: the thing has to be perfect—as
close to ideal as they can get, just like TV food. There is no room for a
flaw in this, our sexy silver dream remake kitchen. It had to be returned
and refurbished somewhere larger, else. But it would return anytime,
they said, and we must be on the lookout for it, and when it comes, it
will be—at last—Just Right™.

Just Right™ is the registered trademark of our major sponsor. It is a
slogan I'm sure you've heard; they are famous for their many sales. They
have as many sale days per year (just under 180) as retailers are legally
allowed in Michigan (any more and you can't legally describe them as
sales). Though the lawyers will probably redact this, you should know
their stuff is mostly crap. It's all veneer.

Possibly our dent is due to manufacturing error, or else it's due to
sabotage. This is one way to explain it. There are forces in our neighborhood that watch over us, are jealous of our new kitchen and soon-to-be
television time. There are also other forces who are happy enough to
say they know us, that they knew us before our big splash, our crash
into and across their screens and digital video recorders. We have had

these forces over to our house for dinner before. We have cooked them veal, and eggplant, and pork butt, and potatoes mashed with garlic and chopped rosemary. We are grateful for our friends, for those who will continue to support us. Still other forces—the authorities, for instance—may want to keep us out of the media. I am sure we are important, our names somewhere inscribed on paper.

Official meetings occur throughout the neighborhood every couple of weeks through the Neighborhood Association. These take place under cover of early darkness. Everyone is welcome, but not everyone is invited. These groups are small. You can go to them and ask for a low-interest loan to do work on the exterior of your house or fill in your backyard like a grave with a ton of fresh topsoil. You can go to them to talk about the recurring problems with tenants down at the end of the block, as in they sell drugs, as in cars come by and park for just a minute or two nearly every night, all night.

The forces that operate against us behind the scenes are happy to oppose us. They hold grudges. We hold grudges against them for calling the city on us last year when we refused to trim our weeds. They hold grudges against us because they think we—they don't know which one of us, Jennifer or me—are criminals of some kind. And that we will be celebrities, which is one step better. It is true we have many instruments of violence in the garage: axes, bows, rototillers, and cordless circular saws.

They are correct. Both Jennifer and I have black marks against us. It is a good thing that the Television Network doesn't do thorough background checks. Or maybe they do (the contract does not specify—an unusual omission in this otherwise comprehensive document) and we are rubes, being duped for your television pleasure. It is not impossible that there never will be a stove to fill the gap in our kitchen, in our life, and that we are being slowly pushed to frustration and then to violence. Option three: they checked, but our secrets are deep enough to resist this brief incursion. Or maybe we are average in this way, too, with our list of faults trailing somewhere far behind us.

Food you see on TV or on boxes of processed food isn't all it seems to be: it's never real. There is an art to food photography, we have learned from one of the producers of this program, who is also responsible for several cooking shows on a network that you may recognize—he likes to give us the inside scoop, the real shenanigan, whatever that means, to quote him directly. They omit moments in the preparation—all the tiny sloshes and spills. They pump food full of chemicals to make it act and look and glisten just like they want. Food stylists are flown in from Madrid. It is in this way just like embalming.

There have been setbacks in the kitchen completion, as I have detailed, but they are above all Not Our Fault. This has a clause in the contract too. We are victims in this, yes. We are at the Television Network's mercy, or the mercy of the Appliance Company that Holds Very Many Sales and Shall Not Be Named. We are at the mercy of the forces iterated above. This is an important point. The trees are lovely while my wife is sleeping in the slowly growing morning light and I fear the future and what it holds for us. In the winter it is always lighter because what light there is reflects off the snow and into our windows, into our neighbors' windows, whose blinds never close but who are unattractive, so there is only a little pleasure there for us.

We walk around naked, we meaning I.

Let my nakedness be a lesson to them.

I believe our stove is on some kind of mammoth vision quest, like that film we saw in school about the carved Native American (we no longer used the words we used then for things) in a canoe that travels all the way from the middle of the continent of North America out into the sea—as if all Native American crappy crafted crafts aspire to be released into the sea at last. I wonder how much of that was staged. What crap is adult life, I think. Aren't we always being duped. Aren't we always going over the lip of some sky-high waterfall.

Is that a real memory or something reconstructed from assorted real events? The film was grainy, sure, but do I remember the real grain of it or the idea of it—grain connoting age, like sometimes in commercials with their faux-old footage meant to hawk some cleansing agent? Sometimes I get things mashed up in my head. I rely on my wife to remind me which things took place and which did not occur. For instance: Did she take my name when we wed or did she not? For instance: Did we wed or did we not? And who took whose last name? I remember bits and pieces of these things. Her hands. The rings we had custom-made from gold. The cat's claws tucked into my wrist skin in the photograph as she attacks my hand. The swell and swoon of blood. A garter belt draped across a chair. Ashes in a fireplace stirred by wind.

On the internet home page of the Television Home Makeover Show they explain how they have done what they have done. You can go there to see a step-by-step guide to how to do these things yourself if you have a load of cash and tools and no fear of either electricity or gas. They have done more than forty homes completely plus a couple of dozen rooms. It is an impressive operation. Of course they have a book that you can order on the site.

I have met the host of the show, who came through to familiarize himself with the set, as in: his set; as in: our kitchen; as in: our house. He introduced himself and said he was very glad that we were chosen. Jennifer thought he was sexy and she mooned over him a bit. She has a thing for most celebrities. It is something about being the subject of so many gazes, she said. Or maybe it's the teeth. You gain this special glow. She has rules and lists. Whom she is allowed to sleep with without guilt if the opportunity arose. At her insistence, I have also compiled a list, though I find it creepy. Is it just a game, I think.

I have begun to enjoy watching the Home Makeover Show on television. It is almost as if the kitchens I see onscreen are mine. Tele-vision. That's kind of a weird word for us to use all the time. Vision from afar? Like watching my neighbors through their bedroom window from my own through the slat we have turned up just enough to get a view, just enough for plausible deniability. Jennifer says we should get it all on tape for when the two of them finally combust. We should keep it just in case they get famous first and we are left behind.

It is not completely beyond the realm of possibility to say that Jennifer may have sabotaged our stove, as in she might have broken into the warehouse while it slept to hammer on the side of it, or that she way-laid the truck along I-90 somewhere in Wisconsin, as in some deserted stretch of road, as in she may have faked a flat, hijacked the thing, and taken apart its insides.

She was less sure than I that we should accept the Network's offer to redo the kitchen. How did they find us? Why did they choose us? These are things she asked. I think it's Grace, or Providence; they saw something in us, something like potential.

She likes the insides of things—the coils that run the stereo, the entrails of birds we find strewn around the yard thanks to the efficiency of the pack of cats that roam around the place and howl like doom at night, the housing around the pilot light on the water heater, the me-chanics of our neighbors' slowly unspooling, spoiling marriage. She writes down the screaming fights—the exact things they say to each other—as if they are gifts. She is chronicling this thing. I think she hopes (even more than I do) that one of them will hurt the other, that we will have more drama, and that it will be barer to the world. In that case, she says, she has evidence against them both. The wife is dull. The husband's cheating. The wife's family is always there, pressing into the husband's space. The husband is inept. The wife never shovels out the driveway. The husband drinks. The wife drinks too. The husband killed our other neighbor's dog a couple of years ago. The wife does not know this yet. The husband does not know she doesn't know. It was almost certainly an accident, we hope and say. An accident is whatever will become of them. No one is to blame. Or they both are. Jennifer logs everything they do. She takes pictures occasionally and files them away by date and time and incident.

I don't care much for dogs. I don't like to look or think about these things. I am not like Jennifer in this, and I am not always home. My work takes me away from home for days sometimes and it is difficult. It is especially hard to return home knowing that the stove may have been delivered without my presence—that this final act of kindness or what- ever you want to call it was done offstage. Or while I was offstage. I want to feel like I am in control.

So Jennifer may have broken in and crushed the main igniters on the stove to keep it from arriving when I was here. She is sometimes self- ish in this way. I am also selfish in this way. This is why we keep separate watches for the stove, for the slow groan of trucks as they ease their way down our streets.

This is absurd. Will it ever come? That is the problem with rising action, why I hate books. Will it deliver, be delivered, in the end?

My brothers call to ask when we will make it on TV and I have to tell them I can't say, as we are not officially allowed to discuss it. They pester me and ask for further definition. I demur and curse them after- ward. They are okay brothers, even if their debts and desires are as deep as wading pools. Of course they did things to me and I to them when we were young. We traded injuries like baseball cards and ran up our parents' hospital bills. Then they moved to New York and Boston and pursued Important Things. They call periodically to find out when we will be on so they can set their digital video recorders to record it all. That way they can be proud or angry forever in the privacy of their nicely furnished apartments. They can call us to complain.

The problem with our kitchen is that without a stove it lacks func- tion, mechanism. It is all surface shine and gloss. It is not a home but a television set. It could be used easily enough for some new niche of porn. Or: it is a kind of porn.

Is it a stove we are waiting for, or an oven or a range? When I call it a oven, Jennifer corrects me. I know the thing but not the name for it. Range sounds anachronistic. As in: home on. As in: where the deer and Beverly D'Angelo play.

The sponsors call to ask if we have received it, how thrilled are we exactly to have this brand-new post-space-age kitchen, and when they can set up the aftershoot. If I receive these calls I make something up. If Jennifer picks up the phone, she tells them the truth.

I feel sometimes as if I could shed this life, this new wife, this wreath of kitchen things, this set of expectations, this gaping hole in the place of the stove, and all I have accumulated—collected true and reproduction memorabilia—like an exoskeleton and leave naked, fresh, and pink into the winter.

Would I go back to what I did before, as in theft, as in serious theft, as in before we designed our shiny new lives? This is what I did for years before I met Jennifer and our lives transformed like energy from potential to kinetic: I stole and sold the things I stole. Mostly electronics when I was younger, but then I found my way to words: I am a professional plagiarist. I run one of the websites you see demonized on the television news that buys students' papers and makes them available for download for a price. We will make over your composition grade and make you happy with your life again.

It is not as profitable as you'd imagine, so I also do some freelance work, passing others' words and ideas off as my own in (mainly) academic journals. There's a little bit to be made here too. I have a hard time understanding some of the more academic language, and what it exactly means, but the surfaces of it glisten, are attractive, worth money. They carry a lot of information. There is nothing wrong with profit. Ask my brothers or the producers about this, but do not mention my name.

I hope this does not make you think badly of me. I am not sure why I'm telling you this at all. The lawyers will, no doubt, redact it before release, so I suppose there is a safety net. Which is why I speak so freely.

I feel sad for you who will have to read this abridged: imagine how much better, more revealing it was in its truer form.

All of the other appliances work. This is not some kind of joke where everything is rigged to fail, though I have thought that before, that we are on the pointy end of some long existential stick.

Tsunamis come halfway across the world and tear one hemisphere to shit, and it is morning and Jennifer is up, and we wait together. She is stunning in the morning when she's lazy. There is mail for her. She is an Actual Writer, meaning that she uses her own words and ideas—she likes the insides of things, as I told you. Any news on the stove, Steve? she asks. And that answer is no. We both know it but feel compelled to ask each other. They said it would be another week before the new stove arrived to replace the old and busted, dented, somehow incidentally injured stove, but their proclamations are suspect. That is: they are shiny shit. They told us it would be half a year, and then a truck showed up a day later with an appliance for us. But it was the wrong stove. We do not want black or the cream color that is so popular now called bisque. It must be as white as a breast in Edgar Allan Poe or brushed and stainless steel, polished up to reflect the rest of our New Dream Kitchen. They had to take it back. There was confusion. Our stylist and makeover specialist called back to apologize both to us and to the Company. There was a mix-up on the line. There was a mix-up on the customer service end of things. He was angry, said he wanted this just to be over. And so it was—the truck took the thing away and left us with the wound, agape, again.

The massive waves and aftershocks from the quake are terrifying on television with its lower resolution. It does not look as real as it does in movies, but that they say it's real makes it that much more so.

What are we doing with our lives? I say.

Jennifer does not respond.

She is furiously taking notes.

A fracas has begun next door.

After I have slept for three or four good hours, I go down to check. The stove is not yet there. Jennifer is not beside me on the bed nor is she at the window with her notebook. She is not anywhere inside the house. I do not panic. She is often gone when I wake up. It gives her pleasure to confound me in this way. She could be anywhere—the dry cleaners, the bait shop (she fishes avidly—one of many Authentic Things she likes to do—so this is a real destination for her), the library, or down by the docks. There is no note. The neighbors are quiet. I make coffee in the machine that both grinds and brews it from whole beans on our voice command.

Is it wrong to say then that I make coffee? Then: I initiate the coffee's preparation, most of which is completed by the machine. Still, it requires my voice to make it go.

There is a truck outside and it is pulling in. Will it stay or will it go? It is unmarked. I have twins: desire for and fear of the sight or sign of blood.

There have been no calls, so it cannot be the stove. Unless: Jennifer answered the phone but let me sleep. Unless: she went out and got it somehow, brought it home herself as if it were a pelt.

The truth is that any day could be the day. Our driveway serves another house. All driveways serve another house—the house that we inhabit and the house that we imagine. I will have to wait and wait and watch.

No—it is a moving truck, I see. Men get out and patrol like bugs up to the door next door. One or both of them are moving out, I realize, with relief. There is nothing to come between us and our future anymore.

Jennifer will be pleased at the outcome of this little drama.

Some mornings I think of myself gleaming on TV from space. All our television is refracted up there somewhere, midbeam, between satellites, and where am I, which is to say, where will I be, in it—that stream of dots or bits and such—will I be at once in more than one time zone, will I be on the edge of our great new tile floor flickering on the border of your screen?

I think of the world asleep and roaming free in dreams.

A touch of snow floats down from the sky like television static.

I think of my wife out there somewhere and the one I buried just before her. I think of the hundred thousand women everywhere at this moment, at once, looking through their screens at me, fingers resting on their engagement rings, deciding whether to give away their names.

Opportunities for Intimacy

It is not as though Shelly fears waking up surrounded by the dead every morning, exactly, since the dead are in every way natural; that is, it is to be expected eventually by the time starlight makes its way from us to the next star over, that we will all be gone, vanished into a point or a line in an epic poem or the great whatever. And she is not squeamish about these sorts of things—she's seen bodies, for God's sake; she's seen hundreds of them, been down to the morgue for identifications, seen them cut up like pumpkin pies for medical exploration. She's walked through the bisected cow behind Plexiglas that caused such a stir at the Tate Gallery in London years back. She's buried her father, a half-dozen friends, and a number of animals—a couple of cats, a dog, twenty-one goldfish, two ill-advised rats, and a barracuda that lived less than a week. What Shelly hates—and this is why she sometimes panics in moments like this, lying next to her lover in the platform bed, the comforter wrapped around her like she is a mummy, hoping (and almost praying, even) for her to breathe, to exhibit some sign of life—is the thought of sleeping an entire night with a person without realizing that they are dead, that they are no longer a person at all. What would this, what does this say about her, that she would even wish them dead before sleep found her so she could tell in advance and do something, take on the immediate heartbreak instead of postponing it awfully until morning?

This happened to her once, years ago, with her cat Rotato, so named by a girlfriend because of his fatness, after that As Seen on TV gadget that peels potatoes for you as it rotates like a magic ball, available then and even now for the unbelievable price of $19.95. Rotato passed in his sleep, and worse, in her sleep, and by the time the sun hit the two of them from the edge of the world again he was stiff and still fat and had been silent, unmoving for hours. The girlfriend was absent for this, and came back a day later from a spring break trip, to the bad news and a very slight measure of guilt, as she had always said that cat was too fat to live. And please get it straight, because she doesn't fear death. This is why she is so good at her job—she tells this to herself as she's dangling off an overpass, the front of her car teeter-tottering, nudging out above the oncoming traffic just north of Ames as I-35 passes through Iowa on its way north to the land of Big Ice or south to the big wide angry of Texas. There's some lesson here about balance. Fulcrums. Something to remember from the semester of physical science in ninth grade. Simple machines and what is meant scientifically by the word *work*.

This is perhaps a result of an unusually drunken night and one too many of her lover Sandy's *Reader's Digest* "Drama in Real Life" columns that she collects, that she posts on a floor-length bulletin board as evidence of Angels in Action (Sandy's words, not hers—Shelly does not go for this crap, and the sentimentality of this lame shrine is sometimes in fact held against said lover, as is her actual subscription to *Reader's Digest*, even if it was the result of a teenage lifetime gift subscription. We all have these lists, Shelly tells herself, that we compile for some future use when inevitability eventually happens, and everything will be finally somehow held up to the light and weighed against us). The drinks were the result of a minor fight, a spat, even, sounding like they're a married couple or something with shared accounts and matching duvet and bedskirts from Bed Bath & Beyond. This is the result of the sort of conflicts most couples have—the minor schisms, the revelation of what two people simply don't like about one another, that in this instance led Shelly out the door in anger. This is the result of years of emotional training and of a complicated Rube Goldberg series of actions that has brought her to this point, tipping out across trucks thundering north filled with stinking compartments of chickens or lazy honking hogs, their snouts poking out through slats like stumps after logging.

This work—and she only remembers the definition vaguely, as in there was an explicit definition, but she doesn't remember what it was, per se—should have stuck with her in physical science, but there were other things happening at that time in her life, her father just dead in his easy chair, luckily not while she was sleeping, and so science didn't get the attention it should have, and thus she doesn't know exactly what to do and how to solve the problem. Do you pitch forward or back? It seems obvious, but she remembers something about counterweights from a story problem, some kind of Train A is leaving Minneapolis loaded

with a ton of hay and traveling west at forty miles per hour. It was always
some oddly low number, meaning don't trains travel faster than cars?
Meaning they do in Europe, she thinks, but not in Iowa where Amtrak is
liable to show up five hours late if the train shows up at all, and the first
time Shelly had to drive down an hour south of Des Moines to pick up
Sandy—her real name, not short for anything—and Shelly had to wait
five hours for the thing to arrive and all there was to read were magazines called *True Confessions*, which, while erotic, were almost certainly
untrue. She thinks to herself that this wheeling mental process she's
engaged in means that she is, perhaps, in shock, that the drinks and the
skid and the guardrail impact have combined to addle her. She knows
this much.

The work Shelly does is about living, not dying. This is an important
point. She breaks the news to patients who have come in for HIV test-
ing (or who sometimes come in for something else, but subsequent tests
turn it up). All positive tests are referred to her because she's good,
because she does not fear death, because she has—as those she works
with say—a gift for delivering this kind of news. Because Shelly is in her
way unflappable. A real one of a kind, and most people couldn't bear to
do it, they say, and they don't understand why it doesn't bother Shelly.
But it's true, it doesn't. Sometimes she gets angry when Sandy refers
to her as the Death Nurse, even when she knows she's joking, because
this is a concern, that the patients will find out which nurse handles
all the bad news, that they will find out and be able to divine (or even
avoid—and patient care is all about bypassing defense mechanisms)
the nature of their news. To this end, she handles other cases, too, and
there aren't as many HIV cases here in Iowa as there are in the bigger
cities, so she would estimate that less than thirty percent of her cases
are concluded in this manner.

So when she herself is up against the actual thought of death—here
precariously caught between the two car seats like in some kind of
melodrama (it would be better if she were tied to the train tracks in an
old-timey dress, kicking—now that's almost hot, she thinks) and waiting
on either rescue or doom, she thinks she's lucky to be the one to bear
this burden and keep it from another Subaru, the grocery and Microsoft
edition, one with a passel of kids therein, or one with a heavy-hearted
couple who had just lost a child, who might have both more and less to
live for, gearing up to try again but each secretly fearing the same result.
Shelly's willing to take a certain amount of weight, of pain and suffering,

upon herself. She's like one of those self-flagellating monks. She is stronger, she thinks, than some.

Certainly she is stronger than some of her patients, one of whom—when told the Bad News—took off running at full speed through the labyrinthine hallways, through the waiting area with its recycled magazines, in fact, knocking a child over, and out into the street through traffic: running full-out away from the news that people equate with either shame or death or both, as if she could outrun microbiology. After sharing a brief stunned moment with a passing nurse Shelly took off running after the patient, and who knows what the other patients might have thought. Finally she caught up to the patient eight blocks later under the shadow of an abstract sculpture that adorns the grounds of the Iowa state capitol building. She had stopped, obviously out of breath or maybe just out of ideas, and Shelly collided with her, caught her in an inadvertent hug, normally not part of Shelly's range of human responses to these situations, but this was not a moment anyone could consider normal, and so Shelly held on to her, and they shared this moment while maybe two dozen bicyclists came out of nowhere and flowed as a group, a school of glittering spandex fish, around them and then just as suddenly disappeared.

That's what you missed, Shelly thinks, the you being the other nurse who didn't run after them: you missed that meeting, that pocket of emotion. We have treatments, Shelly told the patient. It's not the death sentence it used to be.

In her last job before this one, she handled 911 calls. As such this predicament should be familiar. Shelly knows that she should have a cell phone, and it should always be charged, and what the costs are for those who aren't prepared. And she does have one, but it's dead. She let her account lapse a day or two ago. Who could she call except for her lover, who's sprawled out on their bed, hopefully breathing, and angry at Shelly for Closing Things Off As She Always Does. This is why Shelly was out getting drunk. You need an outlet, she thinks, and sometimes it's the bleary pause of alcohol, and sometimes it's lightning striking in the middle of a field and setting the thing ablaze and calling the police because you forgot what the fire department number was in that moment. You need some way to siphon energy away from you, to get beyond yourself. She drank, went to the firing range to blow the faceless faces off silhouettes, and was on her way back after the liquor and the concentrated bursts of violence when she swerved to avoid an animal in

the road and skipped into the guardrail, which, while keeping her from
entirely sailing through, did partially give way, which explains how she
got into this story problem of a mess.

Someone in oncoming traffic must have noticed her predicament
and called the police, who will respond quickly, she thinks. She did the
911 job for five years, which no one ever believes, because the average
tenure of 911 operators is less than a month. You do hear some real
emergencies in 911 calls, but mostly it's the usual weirdness: people calling because they fear they've been poisoned by their spouse, or somebody's got six lures caught in the skin of his hand, or somebody is in
the house, and it's not some sex game this time, they swear, so please
come quick. Nine times out of ten it's stuff that should go to the non-
emergency line, but it doesn't have a snazzy number like 911, so here
we are. The other one of out ten was where it got fucked up: husband's
caught both his arms in the thresher; he's coming for me with a gun
or a railroad spike; or more often it was just fragments of agony and
confusion, barely understandable—people are not articulate about their
terror, their pain, when put on the spot. People wheel and spin and kick
out into space. And there's nothing to do but wait on the line with them
or until the phone goes dead, is replaced in the handset, and then hope
for some kind of timely intervention.

«

Someone, as it turns out, is about to intervene on Shelly's behalf. Here's
Joseph, sixteen, the owner of the animal—an armadillo (pretty weird for
Iowa). Really, he would call himself its friend, not its owner, though it
makes for an underwhelming friend, since it's not particularly pettable
or affectionate. But it's certainly not a *possession!* Joseph is about to
come up from the field of swaying corn that he was detasseling, a thank-
less and mostly awful job that he took to make him enough money
to Get the Hell Out of Iowa. He brought his armadillo, whose name is
Hank, in a cat carrier with him to work. When his supervisors called
it a day but told him he could do some overtime if he wanted to and
left him alone in the quickly darkening field with just a floodlight for a
companion, Joseph went back to get Hank out and let him have some
fresh air while he worked.

Like Shelly, Joseph is good at his job even though it sucks. His father's word for it, not his, since Joseph won't complain: this is the most
money he can make doing anything legal at this age in Iowa, and while

the work is hard, so is Joseph, or so he supposes, and he has something to prove. If he doesn't make it out of here, he thinks, he'll end up de-fenestrating turkeys in one of the giganto turkey barns around here, the new and more humane way to kill the birds that he'll invent when on the job—no blade involved, no gas or crushing blow, just their first and only opportunity—though somewhat attenuated—for flight. He tells himself: you get to go out on top, you assholes! Well, even in his fantasies in Iowa, at best, he's inventing methods of dispatching poultry and not doing anything really interesting. He knows it's bad for him, the state's huge brain drain—all the best students and professionals emigrating out to other—if not better—possibilities in other states with flashy names like Illinois. He could live in Wrigleyville and watch the tourists stream in to watch the Cubs. Or he could work in Texas on one of the oil derricks that he has heard infest the sections of beach that have not been turned into condo-land.

Joseph is repulsed by turkeys, the bumbling birds that his family slaughters for a living. They are hard to love en masse: their strange desires and the awful smell of tens of thousands of them congregated in close quarters. Why turkeys? he's asked his dad, and not gotten a satisfy-ing answer. At school he's known as the Turkey King, The Golden Turk, El Turkamauga, and jokes are made about his smell, which, to be fair, is not good, though not on account of turkeys. He's not gone through anything worse than any other teenager, of course, but it seems pretty bad to him, and in his very darkest moments, he's even contemplated what he could do with his father's gun. He knows it's a wrong thought he's having, and it's not persistent, but it's scary how powerful it is when he's in its grip.

He would never do it. He has restraint, and that's the difference, he tells himself, though if his father knew he'd contemplated it, he'd be terrified, and that's one reason why he's working late, why he's proving something by being overproductive, by emptying himself into sweat and work and corn and supremely itchy skin.

Hank freed himself, it seems, and scuttled out into the corn—these things are way smarter than they look or have a reputation for being—and upon discovering this, Joseph had to run through the rows of corn shouting. He became more and more desperate, since he had to have his armadillo special ordered in the pet shop here, and this fact, when it got out, contributed further to his reputation for stink and weirdness at school. There was No Way, he told himself, that his armadillo would

get away from him, and when he finally traced its path out to the road
he feared the worst for Hank (he's heard that in Texas some citizens
run down armadillos for sport), but when he cleared the wall of corn, he
saw Shelly's predicament first, and only then saw Hank, balled up and
stunned by this near miss, and scooped him up, then looked into the
wreck, feeling something sort of like astonishment. Here, he thought,
was a thing he in some small way caused to happen, even as he knows
it's not properly his fault. He holds his breath, his Hank, and thinks of
what he will do next.

«

About twelve thousand feet above this threesome, a plane drops through
the base of the sparse clouds that tower over the state at night, starting
its descent into the bore of the Des Moines airport. No one is waiting
there for Donald, who toys with his wedding ring, thinking about what
that traditionally means in stories, now loose on his finger since he's lost
so much weight in the past six months—nearly a hundred pounds down
from his earlier mass, which defined the American obese, and even now
down close to three hundred pounds he still had to buy two seats on the
little jet, knowing that he wouldn't fit in one, or that he might but that it
would inconvenience his seatmate, and he's loath to do this, especially
now that he's on the slide toward slim and the kind of physical beauty
and bodily control that he has so long admired in others. You see them
on the television all the time, and six months ago he decided that what
he needed, what his wife and he needed, was a change, was more control, was more constraint on his various appetites, so he took action—at
last he took action! And lo, here he was, returning: a changed mind, a
changed man.

From above it seemed the same. Down in it, it was easy to forget how
small it all was, but then you didn't get this perspective very often. It sure
seemed big enough up close.

Their marriage, he felt, might be on the ropes, but what marriage
wasn't? He was on the verge of becoming that other kind of American
grotesque, the lonely divorcé, and this is what he hated most of all, living up to what the world thought of him. Two of his coworkers referred
to theirs as starter marriages, only probably as a joke. He looked down
at the evening landscape below gridded out by the highway's lights as
the plane banked toward the city and the future. His truck was there,
in hock, in the airport parking lot, and he would return to his wife, who

was thinking of him now, perhaps, if she wasn't out at the bar where she threatened to pick up men while he was gone. He thought this probably a joke. He hoped it was a joke, but their jokes had acquired an edge in the last year, so it was hard to tell. He could not count that possibility out: Would he find her home when he got home or would he not? He was thinking of her thinking of him and of fireflies in Iowa fields in summertime, where everything grows tall enough to keep everything obscured forever beneath corn, if you get away from the cities and out into the silence, whether you come via anger, exhaustion, desperation, or accident.

In the meantime, if he squinted, maybe he could barely make out the shape of Shelly's predicament, not that there would be anything he could do about it from up here. But maybe witnessing the rescue would mean something to him.

You should know that evening fireflies in a field just outside Ames constitute a happening. How can I tell you what it's like to be so surrounded, illuminated by a thousand LEDs, like some kind of rock show Providence, some crazy and perhaps meaningful earthen low-lying constellation? They wouldn't be out just yet. But in half an hour, as Donald drove the long way home through the fields, they would come alive around him.

Did Joseph know what time it was? Did Shelly? Did it matter?

Let's press pause on them for a moment and let our Donald land, deplane, walk sweatily through the airport, and find his truck. Let's let the sun go down a little and give him a head start. Shelly, Hank, and Joseph can wait there for a moment until he clears the corn and sees them. Hopefully he'll slow and pay attention, lend a hand.

From here you can almost see a glow, a starting, there, an emanation in its beginning stages. It's all beauty or potential from this far out, everything quiet, so simple, a story problem with an answer. Maybe Donald, slowing and seeing the scene unfold in front of him, will feel like he's finally part of something he can change, and not just feel insulated from it all in glass or truck or love, in physics or corn or carbonite, not just in his own habits and loosening flesh, but that he is porous to it, to all of it, and even if it's like Homer's comparison of bloody battle reduced by distance to swarming bees, an epic simile, it's his simile, his chrysalis, something for him to emerge from when he's ready, and hopefully he's ready now to see, if not to help, as the stars come out above and the stars rise up around them all, and Hank unfurls and Joseph speaks and

Shelly steps out of the moment of her shock and teetering car and they all stand there for a minute in the confluence of lights and agree with me that sometimes, without regard for your predicament or prognosis, a thousand bioluminescent winged beetles are—or should be anyway— just about enough.

The Gnome

It started curled up in a little story I overheard: the one about being on drugs out in the woods and finding a disabled kid and bringing him back to your camp and feeding him, believing in your altered state the kid was a gnome. Well, I believed in it and told the story to my husband and his friends on more than one occasion. I kept telling it. I clearly loved to. I couldn't tell you why. I found out several months later that it was an urban legend and felt the fool, unsure of whether I should tell them this or not. You know a story's good when it will not abide its end, when it feels like a secret you might keep from your husband and your kid for a very long time indeed. How else to explain how it broke through the retaining wall that kept me from sleep and then took over my dreams—I know it's boring saying so, but it's true; you can't control what holds you when you sleep. It even began to perforate my daily interactions.

Everywhere I went I began looking low and under things for evidence of other lives. Do you know how in the grocery wine aisles wineries have to pay for better placement, at eye level and the shelf below? So all the wines on those shelves—the ones you think you want, the ones most people buy—aren't as good as you think they are. They're the wines they want you to want, and they're never weird or interesting; they're just wines, and if you want those wines, even or especially knowing this, that says something about you. So the wise know to look at the bottles that are a little harder to see, top shelf and bottom shelf, that don't present themselves as obviously. I wondered what I had been missing with my eyes up where they always looked, where the marketers knew I looked.

That new looking action felt like a secret, like I was getting away with something. Or getting filled with something new. One house I walked by on my daily walk had a little gnome head at ground level, underneath an unruly pile of marigolds. I'd never seen it until I started looking down. I must have walked by it ten thousand times. Was it just the head, I wondered, sitting atop the dirt, or had someone buried it up to its neck and left it there? And if so, was it for punishment or pleasure? Or had it burrowed down itself and felt comfortable there or was somehow trapped by domestic magic?

They are known to live for centuries, if you trust the lore. Possibly the yard rose around it: possibly it had always been there. Or the intense rains of last week had exposed it. It did have the look of something that had been there a very long time, like before this neighborhood with its racist charter and its specs about acceptably historic paint colors: the gnome's red pointed cap was mostly bleached now. I told my husband over dinner that a gnome was buried in the yard. That one down right across from school, I said, that we always walked by when we took our son on walks in the evening. Which one? he said. The one with the bashed-up fences that looked like there was always something in there trying to get out. The one with the window into the bathroom where they should really shut the blinds? Indeed. A gnome? Like a garden gnome? I don't know, I said: just a gnome. Yea high? Red hat? Jaunty bastard? he said. Abouts, I said, and once its hat was red. Now it's not. Then it's a garden gnome, he said. He went into an explanation about taxonomy that I ignored.

I was thinking about the thing instead, how old it might have been, how many lives it might have seen elapse without its owners knowing: that's a kind of magic. That's just weird, he said. What kind of people would have a thing like that in their yard? I didn't tell him that it had consumed me, thinking about it. And, more, that I wanted it, wanted to bury it in our yard, for it to have a space in our lives. And I knew I'd soon have to come back and dig it up. Its pointed cap came to mind when I was trying to think of other things, or not to think of anything, like trying to banish an unhealthy fantasy during sex so I could just get off and reassure my husband that he still had it, so he'd finish and I could get on with my evening of thinking about small things. That had become what sex was: a reassurance, a passing between us of something small but important. A relief, too, I guessed. He'd gone on a tangent about his suspicions about the house, how the owners always gave him a weird vibe, the little girl who lived there and how she always looked haunted playing in the yard, and how the dog would come and go, be there for a week and then be gone again for a month. Like where did it go? he wondered. Plus it seemed too large for a yard that small. And it had trashed the fence with its curiosity. Maybe, I said aloud, the dog had dug up the gnome and been banished for it. Or buried it, he said: like a bone.

He was starting to get it, I thought, maybe. So I set it for him as a test, and even as I was doing it, I knew it wasn't wise, to treat a marriage like this, to set traps within it. How well could he understand my desires? And why was it important even? I didn't know. Would he pass by the thing on his long run tomorrow and bring a gnome back home to me, or better, bring this gnome, the thing itself inside our house or our yard so we could use its pull for good?

If he did, then it meant he felt it, too, its importance to our lives; then it meant it had wound its way inside him, too, like a little worm invades a world and soon multiplies and has to find a bigger one to live. This is what I wanted to say to him: I wanted him to see more of the world than he did. He was focused on what he thought was important. You couldn't blame him for that. A life slides you in a slot and you wear a little rut and it gets deeper so that you start to see what you want to see and nothing more. The middlin' wines on the only shelf you see: they're pretty good; they do the job. It wears on you, all that other seeing, all that reckoning with all of it, choice, infinity, I thought, and it was easier this way. I had the bandwidth for so little what with the son and walks and lack of sleep and with the death of our beloved pets, all four within a year, like after the first went the others just gave up and stepped out into nothing.

But it was stronger than I thought: the story. The thought of the gnome down in the ground out in the neighbors' darkened yard.

The night progressed. My son yelled a couple of times and woke me up and I couldn't get back to sleep after the latest round of soothing. Where had I even overheard the gnome story? I couldn't remember anymore. Now that I knew, why hadn't I told my husband it was not true? It seemed secondary to the bleached thing itself. I could see the moon through the skylight. Surely it illuminated the neighbors' house as it did our own. I heard the buzzing of another neighbor's drone and watched it hover over the pool next door, the one where the teenage girls lived and you could feel their evenings trembling with possibility. I wondered: What could you see from there? At night especially?

I thought about our marriage. It meant something, but what it meant I was still not sure. That meaning had been hanging over us for twenty-one years waiting for a sign like this. This was a door. This opened to another life. I give us two days to go through it or one of us would disappear.

Our Song

The best instrument for the music of loss,
which is the best of all music, is a woman's voice.
—Rick Moody

I no longer believe in memory and don't believe in fire. I hold my hand to the simulated flame and anticipate the pain. Even though it's digital it still hurts. It still adds up. All pain adds up eventually until it breaks you. It wires into the nerves, which triggers the flinch, so when I want to do it again—to thrust my hand into it to remind myself how the unreal feels—I don't, not yet. I'm not sure I'm up for it. I'm trying to test my response: Is it consistent with the one just a moment ago? It's fake, but what kind of fake? I want to know. Caribou sees me hesitate and laughs, deservedly so, with the awkward repetition of a loop.

Just because I know it's not real doesn't make it not real, doesn't make it not hurt. Caribou's not real either. She wouldn't understand. She's been my companion for this extended recon, but she's not here, not exactly. I mean, she's present, but when I push on the thought I have to admit that she's not here, not like me. Still, I respond to her like a little twitch. I can see her heartlight give a signal and I find myself blinking back. My heartlight clicks out a message in return. It says *I'm glad we're here together.* It says *it's almost time to go home.*

There seems to be no way up to the surface from this system. I thought there was, and Caribou said so too; we'd observed all the signs: light seeping into the room through seams where light would not naturally occur, like out of the back of a book on a shelf, for instance, or from a toilet lid, and so she thought that this room could lead us into the upper level where we knew we could exit without blowing up the contract, and that was why we were exploring this set of rooms again.

I for one am getting tired of this subdivision: it's just a bunch of passages that interlock and churn at the same set of difficult, knotted-up memories. We mapped all of them and double-checked our work, except for this room, hoping that on the first pass we were wrong, that we would find an exit here. It took almost a day. So we're down to this, or else we have to backtrack even farther.

Here's the flame again. I know I have to put my hand back in and so I do. Caribou's mouth goes *oo oo oo*. I wince and wait for the signal to recede. As if to fill the space where the pain just registered, I laugh at it: doesn't mean it's real, I say. It's not even realistic. See here? You can't see pixels; the system's too sophisticated for that, but the flame patterns are preprogrammed. The apparent randomness, the occasional little flare-up, is on one of four overlapping loops. When you've worked on fire you know the tricks. We watch and it repeats, a heartbeat. See? I say. Caribou looks at me as if to say what do you mean by real? She holds the look for a second longer than is comfortable. We're stuck here in this anterior passage, which is a phrase I only believe I comprehend. Underneath? Outside? Interior of an ant? But it's identified on the work order: anterior passageways B142–171 and connective: workup, map, differentiation, emphasis on error.

I place my hand against the wall. Underneath I know it's flat and colorless—that's how all of this is, just flat and colorless, wireframes, basically—but it looks and feels exactly like carpeting. I think they called this style *shag*. I blink. It's a goldenrod color that I call *nausea*, and I can't believe they ever made this, or that if they did they'd ever put it on the floors much less the wall. Why would you carpet a wall? I suggest a fact-check on both coloration and the installation, but Caribou, consulting the databases, says it's possible: there's a color called magic pumpkin that was actually used as far back as 1972. People used it on walls sometimes to deaden sound or just for how it looked. Okay, nix that note, I say. We move a little farther in.

We're in the client's father-memory. This whole area smells like smoke. It looks like smoke. You can see it curl and get moved around a little in the air. And here he is in a wingback chair, the wing almost as wide as the room from this perspective, the father—not just her father but the very idea of father, the big one, the ur, his face transfixed by something we can't see at first. When we get closer it will slowly be be be be be be be be be be (and I have to twitch out of it, that little loop, like a repeating

curlicue in space and time, some kind of glitch, I think, in the approach;
I make a note) eventually revealed: a pornographic magazine. He's reading the Letters section. *Dear Penthouse, you'll never believe this but,* the
first one starts. And even though I know it's not supposed to be arousing
it still gets a little circuit started and I jump.

The client is thirteen in this memory, meaning we are thirteen in
this memory with her. What does thirteen mean to her or feel like
to her? Well, it's uncomfortable, like a little crawling in the skin or a
song we once liked that won't go away; she doesn't feel like she fits in
here—maybe anywhere. A warbly bit of a Christmas carol plays from a
speaker we cannot see. The corridor is colder than you'd expect, like
there's a window open, or a draft, though there's no windows or doors
except the door we came in through. I note the disconnect. Like her,
we shiver. Looking down, I see I'm wearing a long T-shirt with a palm
tree on it and some script I can't read. The hall feels like it's a hundred
feet long, and angled strangely, like in the Mystery Spot, an old tourist
attraction up where I am from, in which you crawl around buildings
built so as to seem like you're defying physics: balls roll uphill; kids are
dazzled; they ask questions their parents cannot answer. I'm dazzled
by the wingback chair. It looms above our heads and I get the reason
for the name: it is like spreading wings, though more death's-head moth
than dragon.

The client is into dragons. She has opinions about various colors of
dragons, their desires and powers and histories. She knows what pornography is but this is her first encounter with her father in its context. In
the section we just left she's stashed related memories, so we know her
father was an amateur pornographer with what looked like an infinite
collection that he referred to as The Library. He spent hours organizing
it, and she would go through it when he wasn't home, being careful to
place every title back in its precise place, rewind the tapes, replace the
stray hairs he placed to mark pages against intrusion: even then she was
smarter than he believed; she knew more of his secrets than he knew, so
in this way she had—and still has, in her way—power over him. From
that memory we got shifted into the tapes she later made and how it
felt for her, being recorded like that, on camera, how it reminded her—
though surely she would not admit it and might not even realize it—of
her father's extramarital affairs that she tracked and logged and moni-
tored in maroon-colored notebooks without his knowing, and without
her really knowing why she did it either, except it seemed important to

keep count and to keep track of things, to tally and observe. Eventually she had curated quite a library of his indiscretions.

«

Even when you want to, you can't move fast in memory. You're always slowed to three-quarters speed, sometimes even slower. We're not yet sure why. In extreme cases you can get stuck in super slow motion, like an inch a minute, slow enough to fool a consumer-grade motion detector. I remember one assignment where the whole level—a trauma level, no less—was like trying to run through a pool of oil. We were trapped in there for what must have been hours just doing a quick inventory of one freaking room. It was difficult to breathe. You had to monitor your air and queue up actions like a minute before they were performed. Thinking raced way out beyond movement: the delay was powerfully disorienting. I had to detox after that and take a break in a neutral space, my heart still racing. I'd be lying if I said you get used to it.

I hold my breath and see how long it takes to gasp. I ask Caribou if she can confirm that this one's running at about a 3.6. It's plenty bearable but the room keeps getting bigger. Everything stretches out to approximate the feel of the experience, not its exact dimensions. Memory's not documentary. We came into our father's study meaning to ask him about a book that we bought at Goodwill about the history of labyrinths, and why they're called labyrinths, for instance, and we can see he's oblivious to us but we don't yet know why. What's Goodwill, I ask Caribou. She says it's where you go to donate the things you have no need of anymore. Possibly apocryphal, she notes; no longer extant. I've never seen one, for sure, but that's not a shocker. I haven't seen a lot of things. So we creep up to surprise him. He gets larger as we get closer, and we can barely peer over the edge of the chair to see into his lap.

From this vantage point you can't avoid the cock. It's just there: an alert dog, a monolith. It's oversized: they almost always are in childhood memories (you'd be surprised about how many cocks you see in memory). But this one's veinless and too smooth: it doesn't look fully real, more like the idea of a cock. As I pay attention to it, it fills in a little bit. Now I see a vein. It's backscattering impressions from other encounters, responding to my doubt.

Caribou's lights click on—of course it's only me paying attention to the cock—and she notes the details of the green-striped couch. She zooms in on its clever patterning, diamonds within diamonds within diamonds, a nice recursion that must end somewhere, at the level of the stitch, but I can't see that close. Perhaps she can. Sometimes I think I know the end of her abilities and she surprises me. The effect is sharp. There are even stains. Touch it and it's plush. My hand almost goes into it it's so soft. She makes a little whir. The feeling of it gets sharper, too, as I run my hand over it, interpolated from other information in the system. As you'd expect, everything gets sharper the closer we are to the client's eye level. The chair is fantastically detailed, for instance: its wood grain, the beads that anchor the fabric. But the ceiling's hazy. Who remembers a ceiling, unless you counted cracks or tiles or something?

«

Perhaps on account of the claustrophobic dark and the smoke and porn, I flip back to Riyadh at this point, 130-degree days burning the sun into you, leaching your will to live. Being outside felt a little like living in slow motion, so you avoided it when you could. When I lived there I never saw real fire except the occasional plume from the derricks that worked far outside the city throughout the night: they flared and waned like embers disappearing behind clouds of smoke. Outside of their constant cigarette smoking, no one there ever burned anything. The whole place felt already burned.

I flipped my days so I'd get up at 4 or 5 p.m. and work my way through the dark, get through the bad stuff before the sun came up. The country was better then. It was still safe for Americans. The patriarch passed after I left, and the ruling family lost control in the revolutions when the price of oil bottomed out. It was always authoritarian but a convenient kind of authoritarian: clean, controlled, moneyed, safe for us. For the Saudi men, it was a playground, a safe world. But for the third country nationals, those not lucky enough to be born Saudi, who immigrated without citizenship, and who worked there for next to nothing, it must have been a terror. I've never seen outright slavery, and as it was explained to me, their condition wasn't slavery, exactly, but it looked to me like I always thought it might: you could tell in their eyes that they might as well have been bound. For all I knew they were. It was hard to ignore.

I was there working in the caves below the bluffs where the servers slept and blinked and sprung to life when one was triggered. I'd never seen caves like that: not just excavated but cleaned and polished so everything shone. Eerie LEDs refracted down the corridors. I got the gig on account of my father, who worked with the US government and knew what I could do. This being a government gig—technically I didn't work for the Saudis, I worked for the US government on loan to the Saudis; on account of the advanced tech we weren't allowed to work directly for foreign governments, even friendly authoritarian ones—I didn't have to do much. Mostly maintaining code, building ecosystems, and massaging the root systems that function below memory and enable it. We understood the systems differently then, how they interconnected and interacted. We thought we could isolate one and edit it without disrupting others. This was four years ago.

Our larger task was to cache the collected memories of the aging members of the royal family in preparation for some kind of cryonic sleep. The bloodline was dwindling on account of a shared degenerative disorder. Maybe they could see that their rule would soon come to an end. We never saw their faces in real life: only in memory. One of them had premonitions, we were told, and so we encoded those as best we could. We weren't fully sure that they would work, since we'd never done premonitions before: the circuitry was like memory but we had to bring in a specialist since the mechanisms were just different enough so that our certifications didn't cover it. No one's did, but it was worth a shot, they thought. We had carte blanche, they said. Make it work, no matter the cost.

It's a weird country, or maybe rings of concentric countries each encapsulated by the next: the poor country, the contractors, the rich country, the superrich, and then the family. Or perhaps the encapsulation works the other way around, and the poor country is the largest country, the real country, and contains all of the others.

To be rich is to be weird. You start to want things that don't exist—that can't exist, not yet. What else is there to covet? But in many of the Gulf states there's no limit at all: no media to check you, no fiction of the courts. There are laws and there is money, and the latter bends the former. There's only as far as you believe you can push those underneath you, which inevitably isn't quite as far as you think. This is why power fades. So the family got involved in this crazy project, caching as much as they could of what remained of the elder family members on interconnected, liquid-cooled servers, which is where we came in.

It paid well. It had to. My wife refused to come. I don't blame her. It's not an easy place for women. And she didn't want our son taking cues about gender roles from Saudis. So I was there only a year, not enough to feel like I could ever pick much up from the culture myself aside from the food and a few marhabas and masaalamas, and the electric strangeness of the place. Most of the time I spent underground, and when I wasn't underground I was out mostly at night, moving through the souks and eating foil-wrapped shwarmas in the darkened streets: thousands on thousands of blinking networked lights, wavering in the heat.

«

My father once asked me: What are you willing to wreck to get what you want? By this point his marriage had dissolved. He had "other interests," as he explained, in which we were only secondarily involved. He asked me what I wanted. I said I didn't know. I wanted to say something stupid like "to be loved." He said anything you want comes with a cost, right? He has this habit of saying "right?" after things he wanted me to agree with, so I ended up agreeing before I caught myself, even when I didn't. I was often baffled by his intutions about the world.

I have this vivid memory of his flat mouth against the background of the conversation, which took place in a brightly lit fast food restaurant with a group of children all dressed up like pigs in the background. They were dressed like pigs on account of a pork sandwich that the restaurant had just deployed. The best-looking pig—it had to be a girl, I heard some employee say; I watched the faces fall on all the boys—got a big silver star almost as big as she was, would get entered in the competition to be in the commercial for the sandwich, and would get to eat for free. My father's lips barely moved when he spoke. He once claimed it was on account of how he used to be a ventriloquist and though he didn't do it anymore he found it advantageous in his new line of work to betray as little as possible. He worked on major high-level finance deals that sometimes I would see reported in the papers months or even years later. Companies would split or declare bankruptcy based on what he said and did. One very small country went into receivership and was divided up between its creditors—actually and physically: it was but is no more; now the countries on either side of it are each slightly larger. He was not a demonstrative parent. We don't talk now. We communicate only through books: I send him one. He sends me back another. You could choose to read meaning in the title selection but mostly I think it shows how little he knows about me. Sometimes I get a gig because of him. I can always tell those from the others. The interviewer asks questions from a battery of them designed to make me lose my cool. I've done enough of these by now to know. They want to see just how unstable I'm said to be. I say I'm not unstable. I'm just drawn that way.

«

This section could use a little more heat—not Riyadh heat but a winter holiday heat, the kind you might associate with family and safety if you're lucky. Here it's a see your own breath like a dragon kind of cold, clearly impressionistic, and frankly a nice effect. Rarely does the emotional temperature of a memory manifest itself so literally. And father still doesn't see us. Whatever we do, he won't see us in this memory. It's just watching, no real action—as if watching isn't action. You can feel the action. You can feel just how grinding it must have felt to watch when you're forced to live inside of it.

Still, we're not quite sure what's happening. He's got his magazine. He flips the page slowly to another spread. He licks his hand. These are not pleasant memories. It's hard enough to map the tunnels as we're doing; it would be worse to live them every time we closed our eyes. So much of what we keep is weird and dark and vaguely sex-related—you learn that fast—even if time and distance smooth it out a little. That's what we are, what we're made of, what all of the better parts of us are built on top of. You may not want to visit it—or maybe you do. I can't say.

Yet we encounter little miracles: the detail of the hair on father's legs is spectacular, for instance, how it curls and moves, and you can even find little hairs on the ground from time to time. I hear a little *oo* from Caribou in response—she's noticed, too—and we turn away before we catch him masturbating. We've seen this before, when he's a little older, when the memory is fresher, and we know exactly where this leads.

The problem is the same with all of these reexperiences: they get rewritten from time to time so the maps are only temporary. They're usually stable for a year unless some kind of trauma overwrites them first. We're paid to map them, since the technicians need the maps to simplify their work. I am not supposed to know how they edit the code. That's not my job any longer. My certifications lapsed a couple years back, though I still recognize most of the protocols. That is what they do; this is what I do. There is a line between. It's all in the contract. The better the maps, the easier it is to edit a room's code without disturbing larger narratives. It's like a scan before a surgery. No one sings the song of the radiologist, but it's necessary work. Everything is sensitive. Which is where Caribou and I, professional sensitives, come in.

«

I should clarify: I am real but Caribou is not. Or: Caribou is real but not real in the way that I am. She is a companion-construct, here because the work is real lonely otherwise: the longer you're down in it, the more it unravels your belief in meaning or in meaningful action or in anything. Having someone else helps. Even if she's not real, she's here, and it's easy to fall into the sort of conversation you can have with a comfortable fiction.

I should also clarify: I made a bad decision two years ago that rerouted my life. Because of that I lost my wife. I lost my boy. I lost who I thought I was. Became someone—something—else. We'll get to that. You can't come right at it: like some memories it's too tender to touch directly.

While I'm clarifying, here's my foundational tragedy, as I see it: it's probable that I burned a boy when I was young—a cousin, in the woodshed, badly, with gasoline, deconstructing model rocket engines—but knowing what I know about this world I know I can't be sure. And if I can't be sure, what does it mean that I was accused of it, that as a result my side of the family got disconnected from the other side, me cut off from all the cousins I spent every Thanksgiving and summer and Christmas with, on account of blame and how my parents treated me and how their siblings treated them after the event. What does it mean that I have a corridor just like this that replays the scene for me in my weaker moments? The scene is by now only that: a scene, a little fairy tale I tell myself over and over. I try not to tell it but still I tell it, or it tells itself: The Boy Who Burned His Cousin Badly While Believing He Could Summon Demons with Model Rocket Engines. I don't remember it, not really.

You'd think that doing what I do I'd be able to keep a better hold on all of my memories, that I'd understand them better. That I'd be in control. Nope. I still get flashes of this cousin's face, and then of running into the house, of finding my older cousin who was supposed to be watching us but was instead getting high as was his habit, tuning in and out of playing video games and performing unnecessary repetitive actions like climbing and descending stairs or equipping and unequipping various bits of gear for the sake of it, wondering if somewhere within the game he would discover some secret bit of code equivalent to the sort of cheats he remembered reading about in gaming magazines from his childhood (someone must have discovered them—by sheer repetition, no less), and chuckling darkly to himself at something that was less than obvious to me. I still get flashes of me interrupting his reverie, pulling on his shoulder, and trying to get him to take some action, get off the couch, dude! I need you now, dude! time to hero up! I remember saying (and even now thinking about it thinking what an odd thing that was to have said: did I even say it or did I later invent this bit of wit?), and his shruggy response, like he had been tethered to the television and if disconnected he might wither. And after he was finally cajoled into action how he freaked the fuck out and ran around in circles shouting to some god whose name I can't remember, and how it was me who had to dial up 911 and get the flames extinguished. I remember what it smelled like, that burned flesh, how the mesh shirt my little cousin was wearing got embedded in the burn and even after it was removed in surgery the pattern remained. That pattern is what I remember more than anything else: a diagonal grid with little holes that must have looked hard-core in the 1980s when we believed that was what the future was going to look like: everything mesh and made from plastics, parachuting fabrics.

Everything's still mesh but it's not made of plastics. It's made of memory: little bits of lace, intertwining everywhere. All of it made up of lattices of code. What you see and feel: it's illusion. If you know where to find the seams you can pull them back and see the pulsing fabric underneath. If you want to. If you have the money.

My cousin's still alive. His face still holds the evidence. I'd bet he has a whole complex of corridors devoted to it, to me, to that summer we played together, that summer we practiced incantations and launched rockets into the sky, believing in our futures in spaceflight or necromancy, and how it ended. Demons never appeared to us even after we sacrificed the neighbor's dog. We never went to space. But there was a fire. We summoned mineral spirits and, with the engines, they conflagrated. Gasoline fumes caught and we barely got out alive. I think. I mean I believe. Or maybe I was told. I keep being told. I mean that I really can't be sure anymore and I don't know what that means or how to change.

«

Being inside this thirteen-year-old makes me miss my boy, or the future of my boy. He's not thirteen yet, less than halfway there, but he'll have built up level after level of his own, only some of which I will be in. Children's memories are stronger and stranger than adults' memories, as you might expect. Everything's exaggerated, like in a funhouse, if you've ever been in one of those: every slight and every pleasure, each embiggened. And things interconnect in ways that defy explanation, even when you've been through enough of these systems. Children don't yet have the body of experience that walls off one story from another: instead they mix and bleed. Mapping them is risky work. Because of this we almost never enter someone before they get through adolescence. It's just too volatile. But an adult's memories of childhood are much stabler. Still, they can change—all of us can change, sometimes even without our knowing it—and the labyrinth can shift, get rewritten, with just a chance encounter or a little nudge. What you think is fixed isn't. The brain keeps working until you're dead, and even a little after. Or if you've migrated some of it to the servers it can continue whirring and clicking and rehashing everything it knows for a very long time indeed.

It's particularly thrilling to be nine years old or younger in a memory. Being there you become nine too (or you're superimposed: you can know what you know and think what you think, but you're also aware of the pull of the emotional tenor of the child, which is more powerful than you remember, having lost some of that urgency in your adult life). You can see why some people get addicted to it, reliving at the expense of living. That's one reason why we get sunsetted out after ten years, and get moved from client to client. It's easy to become dependent, to find yourself too familiar, to begin to think of the client's lovers as your lovers, her friends as your friends, her family as your family. You lose objectivity and start to miss things. And the longer you're in strong memories, your own begin to shift. You can't take them on exactly: memories can't straight-up migrate from one mind to another, but you develop secondary systems of them: just as it's possible to confabulate a memory from an experience you've only heard about, over time you can start to build your own simulacra from what you experience in a client.

Some of the client's memories date back before her teens, but they're only useful in how they crosslist and spider underneath the teenage years. No one doubts their veracity. They provide circumstantial evidence for evaluating these corridors. We took a little detour into one where she was four and eating oranges from wide steel bowls. She would keep eating and eating and never get full, her face—our faces—smeared with pulp and juice and building up, layer on layer, like a citrus cocoon.

«

We're not supposed to know about the client. Nothing identifying. None of her data is provided. But you learn fast when you're in the tunnels. You can't help but be the protagonist in the memory. Being this thirteen-year-old watching her father masturbating, you start to figure out what and who she is and how she got that way. She looks, well, not the same now, but it's not hard to connect the dots. She's very well known. She's had some facial work done. The breasts, obviously. If I told you her name you'd recognize it and we could get into the pop psychology, a side hobby of everyone who gets to come down here. Because of this we sign our nondisclosures, which are ironclad and spiked with scary legal language. This is also one reason why we work in teams of two, one human and one companion-construct, since one person's voice can be ignored if we were to break protocol and leak something somewhere later. And who'd believe me anyway? I can't export any evidence, can't take a sex tape back with me. They search and wipe your logs and metadata when you come out, so each time when you return, you're clean: you're new. And so all it would be is whatever fragments I could secret away in my own memory and keep hidden through the cleaning, which isn't much. What I could tell people is worth zilch since I'm easily discredited.

They only employ the compromised.

Celebrity or not, this memory—this is one of the abuse, down that other corridor—is painful to look at or just to know it's there. I knew it was. I knew it was coming, so I've left it for the last. Being inside it is intense: one of the difficulties of the job is managing how easily emotion oozes from the experience, how completely you are filled by it. I'm breathless even pressed against the walls, as far as I can be from the action at the center. The painful thing is how sensuous some of the details are. There's this moment with his smile that's directionless—what could he be smiling about?—but almost loving. A focus on the skin around a mole. The rising of her body in spite of itself. The pointless, undigestible shame. It's basically just a machine, the body. We shouldn't ascribe so much meaning to its automatic processes. How much she hated it—that rising, and how it's become complicated through years of analysis. A snippet of a song comes in and out. It's familiar but I can't identify it.

Maybe "I Love a Rainy Night," I think, distorted and looped, but the more I hear the repeating bit the less I'm sure. I can't quite hold it long enough to tell. I don't know what that means, but I make a note.

The forensic technicians will be here soon to look at the code. Caribou says we've got another thirty-six hours before they arrive, and we absolutely have to be gone or the contract's void.

The abuse scene is the one that leaked, the one we're contracted to investigate. They still don't know how it got out. Hackers, supposedly, but I don't see how you could get that much data out of here what with the built-in controls. Getting in is one thing, doable, since the human mind has its default passwords and rootkits, too, and once you're in it's not hard to narrow down some of the codes and access the protected areas if you know what you're doing and come prepared. But getting anything of any size out of here is beyond my comprehension. They would have had to have a team. They'd have to have had access to her for a couple of days. The client had a security kit installed a year after she got big. I looked at the paperwork on the way down so we could navigate our way through. She should have been secured against intrusion, and it should have been impossible to exit with any data without a fail-safe that would have shut her down for a couple of weeks, and imagine all the attention that would have come with that.

The creepy thing is that people paid for it, this data, these fucked-up memory tapes. It leaked and a lot of people paid a lot of money to access it because of her celebrity, because they believe they can know her through a tape. Maybe they just want to see her hurt. I bet some do. The question is: Was the tape real? Was it a prefab or a plant, as the client's people claimed? How did its details connect or hold up when you pushed on them? This matters in the courts, and for her father, who now stands accused, of course, but it matters more for the narrative her people are trying to make. Even though the client didn't bring forth any accusations at first, when the tape came out it was hard to get around what everyone who cared to could see that he'd done and people wondered publicly why she hadn't come forth, so she had to. Which is ridiculous. Millions of people never come forth with stuff like this—and worse—for a million reasons, many of them good, and all of them understandable if you get to experience what it is like to be them. But online everything gathered steam and now phalanxes of lawyers were involved. Hence Caribou's and my doing this recon as commissioned by the client's counsel. We found some vulnerabilities in security and emotional response; we also found inconsistencies in a few scenes, so we do have something to report along with the maps. I look back at Caribou and she's looking at me, her wide eyes wider than I remember. I see myself in them before she blinks. That's odd, I think.

«

Disturbingly, it's not unusual to experience arousal in a client's memory. Even in the darker corners of these memories, we're always bodies, learning how to be bodies, controlled by subroutines we can barely fathom. So every little interaction—the sound of a hairbrush being stroked through hair—can sear itself in our psyches in unexpected ways. Thus hiccup fetishes, choking fetishes, burning fetishes, fetishes for Santa or for Satan or for girls dressed like demons, for professors or confessors, amputation fetishes, fetishes for fire or being burned, for acting like crash test dummies and being acted on in fantasies. You know how it is. The brain wets down and swallows things in ways the daylight mind doesn't want to have to handle. So it presses on all of this, and each night these corridors go a little further subterranean.

Maybe you're thinking it's like a video game dungeon with nice clean corridors and decorations on the walls: sconces, paintings, chains, whatever. It's more like an anthill than that, more chaotic, with dozens or hundreds of passageways that go up and out and curl around each other, kind of like models of the nervous system, actually, with its nodes and branches, cluster after cluster. The density and patterning vary from client to client, but when you look at the maps we make, memory tends to look like memory, massed and knotted. The lower you go, typically, the further back, so when you're mapping you try to find your way back to the root. It's like being at the dentist when they press on the soft spots of your tooth and when you feel the shooting pain rise up in response you know you've found something you can follow.

Caribou and I came down through an opening from a Christmas six years later, and before I could even mark it on my chart, we could see that our way in was gone. If it gets real bad we could always fail-safe out, but it voids the contract when that happens, and this is an important contract, and besides we never fail-safe out. We always find a way, as Caribou says. We need the contract. We need the money. I need the money. I need to make a point. I need a win.

«

I guess I want to say it's not important what I did. Or didn't do. I can't even be sure I did what my ex said I did, but I did something. Something was done by me. Mistakes were made. I guess we all did some things or else we wouldn't be here spelunking in someone else's fucked-up history. Did or didn't do. That is, I don't believe I really did it. I don't remember doing it. It doesn't seem like something I'd do. It's not my way to respond to barbs with force. I remember having done it but not doing it. Wouldn't I remember doing it if I did it?

They won't say so but all of this, really, any memory, nearly, can be coded and implanted. With the proper privileges you can make most people believe that anything has happened to them. You don't even need to code it, really. They proved this back in the early aughts. You can do it just through intensive interviews. The success rate then was only about twenty percent, but that's a lot of people believing in things that never truly happened. You can always fool some of the people some of the time. Now our success rate is better than ninety-five percent. I've seen it. I can't talk about it here. It's illegal but not unpopular.

It's much harder to redirect a memory if the client is meant to be the actor in the scene and not just the one who's acted on. That requires a complete confab of several interconnected levels; it unbalances whole wings of the ego system. But if you have the money and the time and the permission and don't mind doing it on the sly the services are available—overseas or in portable labs like this one we're in now. We're not supposed to know where it is, of course, but it's obvious we're at sea somewhere. I don't know what else would explain the rocking. Usually those who have this done are those who want to forget—not remember. But forgetting is just another kind of memory, a screen-and-stitch job, and you have to work in something else where the excised stuff once was.

So, I told my wife, if we can do these things—not just if but that we can, and that we do, and that I do—and I know I shouldn't have, but I had to tell her. This complicated things for me with the company and didn't help at home. That we can do them means that we can't know what we did or did not do, to whom, and when and where. It doesn't mean we're not responsible, I know. I was caught in a bind here: I was and was not responsible; if I didn't do it, then I couldn't be held responsible, but was what she wanted for me to be responsible? To evade or take responsibility? I don't know. She wouldn't tell me. All I saw in her eyes was horror, which I took to be horror at the work I did, that I had done these things and developed these beliefs in secret for years, but it was also horror at not telling her, horror at holding these things in even as I held her close, horror at throwing her whole life into question, horror at not knowing this whole world had opened up within me and thus within us, even as we had reproduced, and there was no going back after this point. I had changed. Her sense of me was gone, and in its place there was a wizened, weakened thing.

I couldn't even understand what I had wrought with my actions and then with my omissions. I wasn't even sure that I had done anything at all or that any of us had done anything at all. I kept saying this. I clung to this. I believed it—truly. She said I wasn't fit to be a parent and I wasn't fit to stay with her. That I needed to go away. I didn't know what else to say or do. So I agreed. By then I was in a pretty lonely place, and so I took myself away, ostensibly to try to fix my shit, but I took the silence and the time and loneliness as an opportunity to try to build her something big, to make a gesture that proved not only that I was an actor, capable of action—a protagonist—but that I acted as I always did for her, that I was trying to protect her, not just obscure my own cowardice. I was pretty sure. Knowing what I know makes it hard to live without a certain sophistic streak. She was not impressed by any of my explanations. I knew she wouldn't be, which is why I didn't mean to tell her and she cracked me open like a clam on a rock and there was no gathering all of it back up.

«

The unpredictability of memory and self is in part why you can't operate on yourself. It's not because some kind of time travel paradox arises: after all, what is memory but haunting our own corridors and remaking them, over and over? That happens organically through the process of remembering and renarrativizing: you don't need a tech to do it for you. But to enter in your own head as a tech means you have to take two perspectives in your self at once, and the strain of that potentially blows the fantasy and wrecks the head. It can't be sustained. At least, that's what we know so far. Every so often someone tries to do it: they can't resist. And technically you can. You can do it. Go in and tweak some of your own code. But tweaking that code—and even exploring your levels as the kind of ghosts we manifest as—poses major dangers. It's like a brain surgeon operating on his own brain. Or that's not a good analog at all: it's not brain surgery, or not directly. Brain surgeons actually can op-

erate on themselves, since the majority of those surgeries are automated
now, done by robots with guided lasers that exceed the stability of the
human hand. Plus, brain surgeons tend not to trust anyone else at the
helm when it comes to anything, especially themselves. Still: you need
to have another medical professional present in case it all goes wrong.

You'd have to be crazy to go inside yourself. Most people's brains
can't bear the strain of doubling. So when you're in, you're not a ghost:
you're real. All there. Entire. So there aren't any fail-safes when it comes
to you. Conscious, you're always shifting. You'd be operating without a
net—with no backup and no way out if you got lost or the structure
shifted with you in it.

«

Caribou and I are only paid if we can find our way back out, and we
always do. To fail-safe disrupts the work and breaks the client's brain a
little: it's like burning a man-sized pair of holes right up through everything that might be on top of it, connecting every corridor in unexpected
ways. So we're paid to map and probe and find our way back out without
disruption. The most important thing I can do is to map the catalysts,
those seams I talked about before. Usually they manifest themselves in
light, but sometimes you can find them by noticing repeated symbols or
images, or where the detail is the brightest. When we see a detail that
we've seen in other scenes, we know there might be an opening. It's not
always clear what will lead where. So we handle everything we can in a
passageway. Look at it all. Write it down. Touch it to see what's there.

This is how it works: I grab on to it. If it's a catalyst I can feel it shift. I
get a bit nauseated, as if I've been caught in a lie. I can tell there's something else here, like a doubling. I can choose to follow or leave it be. If I follow it, it's like I go through a door into another room and Caribou comes
trailing after. Usually you can recatalyze and come right back when that
room's been mapped. But other times it's a one-way trip and you have to
find your own way back. The more you know about the systems the easier
it is to predict what might lead where, but it takes attention to catalog all
the stuff. That's where Caribou comes in. Her abilities in this regard far
outstrip my own.

So in this scene I see a teen magazine advertising a quiz: How
Lonely Are You? and when I flip open to that page, it turns out I've seen
it before, in another room off another corridor, and so when I hold it I
can feel there's something here. When I take the fork, Caribou and I get

dropped into a pasture among a whole lot of horses. Caribou calculates that there are eighty-nine. The field is overwhelmingly green. It seems open and stretches on in all directions. A great hay scent is apparent. The horses don't seem to notice us. This is a lovely break from the claustrophobia of most of these memories. The feeling here—and thus the connection—is a particular brand of loneliness. How could you be lonely among all this movement, this beautiful muscle?

As I walk the perimeter I can tell we're still constrained. I can see the field beyond but cannot seem to get away from here. I walk, and it feels like I move, but then I'm no farther from the pasture than I was. I'd be terrified, personally. I should be terrified. These are wild horses, much larger than I am. I'm maybe ten here—I can't tell so easily with girls—with my hands outstretched like I'm a sunflower facing up. I seem to know no fear. I think I've just been left, or perhaps this is some kind of mashup of fantasy and memory. I nod at Caribou. As you might guess, one of the horses has genitals. I really don't want to hold its dick in order to see if it's a catalyst. Of course it is, I tell Caribou, and say right, just chart it. We already know where this leads. We don't need to see for sure. She looks at me. I know we have to, but really I don't want to do it. Instead, I stall. I pretend to be analyzing the scenery in the distance: Is this mountain range familiar? I ask her to check against the database. As we wait it starts to snow. The horses stop what they are doing and look around as if to ask what this stuff is. I hold out my hand. It's cold and my breath steams up. I watch the snow collect. I lean my head back and stick out my tongue. When a snowflake lands on it I see light and vibration, and I take the opportunity to shift out to whatever snowy scene this catalyst reveals.

«

It drops us back into Christmas and Dad is downstairs lifting weights. I can hear the grunts and then a telltale clank that means he's occupied. He's always in a good mood when he's done working out, and then he'll sing for us. He's got a lovely voice in spite of his many defects, and I can feel the anticipation rising in me to hear it. That's one thing Christmas means to the client: her dad singing, the little wings of the bird ornaments on the tree sparkling in the light as they turn. This is a very welcome sound because it means we're back. Outside the window I can see the snow falling. At last, I say, breathing a little easier. I grab Caribou and give her a little hug. She whirs along with me. Mother isn't here either.

I don't know where she is. She wasn't here the first time around and she's still absent in this scene. She's in very few of the client's memories. We've made notes on that, but it doesn't seem especially important.

This is where we entered before the catalyst disappeared on us. I take a look at an ornament almost on the top of the tree. It shows some light. This means our route back out of here remains. There's just one more errand that I need to run before we go.

«

Being here has everything to do with faith: we're here because someone can't believe—not fully, not that kind of solid faith I see (or think I see: every surface concealing a cavern) in, say, the Apostolic Lutherans, the ones who have committed so much to their way of being in the world that you sense that they can't not believe, that they feel like it would mean the very end of them and of the world they've so laboriously constructed around them. They edit their world. We all edit our worlds, but their editing is doctrinaire: certain things are circumscribed by scripture or by decree. Others edit their worlds down by habit, and there's where I start to feel closer to them: What of this world isn't accessible to me without my knowledge because of how I've been accustomed to acting? And then I must admit the possibility that I am who I am, acting how I act, however that is, however capricious and seemingly learned or ruined, because I'm also at the mercy of these chemical encodings. I'm no more free than anyone, even if I choose to believe I am. I have my rooms and corridors, too, and so do you. And the problem is that they're unstable.

Being here also means believing in Caribou, having faith in her wiring, to put it bluntly. She's here to perform calculations that I can't do unassisted and to uplink us to the larger circuitry, which I also cannot do, and the maps depend on a level of precision I can't otherwise get at.

She's a she because maybe of my psych profile or the interviews I went through when I joined, and partly by policy. Studies show it's easier for heterosexuals to believe in a connection to a virtual other if it's sexed, even rudimentarily so, and if it's sexed as the opposite gender. It doesn't speak well for us, put that way, but there it is. They figure that's so because we're more likely to treat the other as a black box, which is basically what Caribou is anyhow, a box with a shit ton of heuristics, and honestly, she can believe, too, she's pretty advanced, she has to believe in what she is and what she's capable of, and that there's something there beyond the programming: she's programmed to have some emergent behaviors;

this is why she's how she is, a little weird, and weird in response to the way I'm weird, since she's my partner in this spelunkery, and therefore reads to me as individual and quirky even and she's easier to love and to believe in, and even knowing that these are expected responses doesn't honestly diminish them that much: it just layers another complexity atop them to navigate, and it's increasingly easy to ignore those complexities when you're wrapped up in a moment as we always are down here and just conflate all of her programming into her, just Caribou, in all of her sweetly digital clicking.

«

I should tell you now that I haven't been completely honest. Or I haven't told you all of it. I knew the identity of the client coming into this job. It doesn't matter if I'd seen the tapes or not. Because her work is so well known and because of the questions that have been floating around the media about the famous tape, I knew it would be her when I got the call and saw the contract terms. I said yes. I didn't have a choice, but if I did I would have said yes.

I never touch the product, but this time while I'm here I am going to make some edits. I'm using her memories as a kind of installation. Don't worry: I've made sure she's insulated. She won't suffer for the additions, nor will she ever know, if I do it well. I'm just making a few edits that will manifest themselves in a future song she will write. She'll believe she'll write it—in fact, she will write the song, it'll all be hers, the melodies, the beats—but the thing will hatch from the eggs I've left, a few bits of suggestive data. I've placed them here for you, my dear, my ex, my former. I know it's wrong to do, but I don't care. Sometimes you do things that are wrong because you care. I figure this is my last chance to make the kind of gesture to prove you can believe in me, that I know what it means to want to be heard like that.

So we move back into the masturbation memory and track back through the corridor toward the complex where the client's song ideas are centered. She doesn't know this: the contract specifies that she must not know. Some believe that knowing where it comes from ruins it, whatever that it is for anyone. But for me it wasn't hard to see: it all comes out of here, this room. As soon as we dropped in here it was obvious, but it took a second pass through to be sure. Catalysts all over the corridor light up: they connect vertically and tendril out into moments from her musical career, right up to the present. It's like the room had been mined a hundred times: I've never seen one like it before, so famil- and so well used. Most of her listeners don't believe she even writes her own stuff. Well, I can tell you that she does and it comes out of here. So few of her contemporaries do. It's hard to believe in anything, even the inconsequential stuff.

these eggs: I mean eggs like Easter eggs. I'm burying them here. It won't take long for them to appear in a song: maybe a month to incubate, maybe a year. I'll be gone by then but you'll hear it one day and you'll think of me: you'll know that I was here and I contributed to this; I de-faced this one memory and did so with your name. It's unusual enough and you're self-conscious enough about it that you'll know it must have been me. Who else would it be? Just wait and see, I mean to say. Just listen on the radio for our song.

Caribou looks at me as I pop the panel off a section—a photograph of two people out along a dock and the sunset stretching beyond them toward infinity—the effect is of these two people being flattened by the sky and sea—I can't tell just which two they are—the client and her dad, mayhap—and I start inserting code. I can tell by her posture that she wonders what I'm doing. This questioning is coded in her. She is not just my partner in this place: she also logs events.

I try to keep the connection hidden as I tweak. All I need is plausible deniability. I tell her I'm checking on some underlying code. This is true. She can also tell when I'm straight-up lying, since she's wired right into me. It's necessary to keep her a little in the dark. If her emotional ba-rometer registers betrayal she'll be obliged to propagate a message out. I'd have to tweak her code first, which I only sort of know how to do. It's possible I'd disable her in the process. It would be difficult to explain to management. So I ask her to check the father's speech patterns against some of the other ones we've listened to instead. I thought I heard a discrepancy, is what I say. We need to track that down. She turns away to listen. It keeps her busy while I work.

We're in one of the sex sections, here in some version of her father's porn library, where most of the client's songs originate, even the ones not obviously about sex. She's alone: there's no father here. We're a little older: sixteen or seventeen, maybe, feeling a little more assured than we are used to. This is a place we've come to often. He's off somewhere un-knowable, so she's left to catalog and to peruse. She could read anything here, do anything here. It's a weird mix of safety and possibility: either way, electricity. You can feel it almost crackle. I thought at first it was fiction—I mean friction, static generating between our ass and the fabric of the chair in the dry air—but it's not. It's something else, excitement literalized. The room is almost fully lit with the seams coming off books all over the shelves and the three screens built into the entertainment center. I put my hand out to them and get a little shock.

Even though the memories are more of awkwardness and archiving than sex somehow this is what she taps into when she tries to write. I don't know why or what to make of that. I don't know how exactly she gets back here or why here is where she goes, but this is where it happens. If I were another kind of person I could disable almost everything in this hallway and render her inert. What would it mean to be someone capable of that? Am I capable of that? I tell myself that what I'm doing here is smaller: just an edit doesn't matter. I believe that. I'm pretty sure I believe that. All I'm doing is adding to the mix. It's like we're collaborating. I should get a writing credit.

«

Death doesn't have to end it. That was the Saudis' idea, why we preserved as much as we could of the royal family. How much of an afterlife could they buy? As it turned out, we could migrate only three of them to the servers with any kind of completeness. That was after an intensive effort that lasted years and is still ongoing, as far as I know. I was only there for one year of it. They rotated all the techs in and out so none of us could feel proprietary. What was there of them—maybe a hundred thousand corridors apiece, judging from the maps I saw—was too immense and complicated to completely port. We had to make decisions about what could come and what would not. I was surprised we could even make reasonable simulacra and uneasy about the choices made: the patriarch, of course, and two of his twelve sons, one of which was the one with prognostications.

We got the outlines of everyone else that they requested, but had to focus on only certain knots of most of them, so they were more like ghosts: they were there if you looked at them from five angles or followed them for five stories (the going standard for a casual facsimile), but beyond that they just turned and disappeared. I don't need to tell you that all of this work has metaphysical ramifications. The philosopher-consultants are paid to sort that out.

The upshot is that it turns out we can preserve a lot of it, what makes you you, what makes you think like you do, feel like you do, hurt like you do, act like you do. Almost all your tendernesses can be migrated to the servers if there is money enough and will. But there's no interface out, no mechanism to interact with the world, to learn, experience: at that point you're disconnected from the world. All you can do is to relive your past and interact with the simulacra in the adjacent suites in ways consistent with your memories and theirs.

I imagine the three of them floating in the cooled towers of the subterranean server rooms, if they're anywhere, playing Go (for some reason they were all in love with Go). I mean they're *playing* playing Go: they're just reenacting former games of Go they've played together, recombining existing things. Maybe they are solving Go eternally, constructing some kind of biological proof. The servers are protected against intrusion and are off the grid entirely. When we're done no one will know that they were kept this way, that they're still out there in the darkness, lit up from time to time by LEDs. In this way they are entombed like pharaohs, surrounded by their familiars and their sigils and their gear. I like to think of them howling at each other's imperfect preservations, stymied by a memory that they know somehow is missing but that cannot form and cannot change, a dead-end passageway, tormented by what they were always tormented by, plus the knowledge of their incompletion. Clearly I still harbor a little bit of anger toward those who can afford the work we are tasked to do.

«

Caribou has finished with her voice analysis and has turned her attention back to me. It's obvious from her eyes that she's concerned. She sends a query and I deflect it. Everything here's a little slower than I thought, so she was able to finish her calculations in the lag while I was still twitching at the panel. I'm out of practice and my certifications are a year out of date, which matters more than I expected. I'm working as fast as I can, but Caribou moves in toward me to register her concern and get a closer look.

As she comes over to record what I'm doing I say oh! look out! and I don't want to do it but I don't seem to have a choice, and while her head is pivoting to follow my gaze I don't mean to do it, and it takes longer than it should, and I'm watching myself doing it even as I'm doing it, but still even I have to admit I'm in the moment doing it: I pick up a book, a big one called *Innocence: The Human Form*, which features, I find out after, soft-lit, arty shots of nude teenage girls. I grab it from a low shelf, hit her with it, and she goes down. I kneel beside her as her eyelights flicker and go dim.

I look away.

I throw up in a trash can that's barely finished rendering.

I tell myself to make a note of its inconclusiveness. Why's there even a trash can in this memory?

I know what I have to do to protect myself, so—tenderly, for what it's worth, and in touching her this way I realize we've never touched before, not really, aside from brushing by each other in slow motion—I locate the seam up where her head meets her neck and slide my finger underneath the flap and flick her into standby and back on. I should have about fourteen minutes before her system will automatically reboot and she'll recognize the outage in the log, so I'll need a story.

I finish up my edit in the room and say *lo, let there be light* as I get the panel on and the room flickers for a second and then lights up, and then I watch as catalysts propagate the edit, each of them lighting up just for a second like I imagine lightning bugs must after mating, or maybe in anticipation of mating. I wish I could share the sight with Caribou. Then I go to work on her. I only have a couple of minutes left.

When she comes back online, I'm holding her. I've made up the scene: bookshelves collapsed, books everywhere, all over the two of us. I've suffered an injury myself, from which the blood has leaked from my scalp over my face. Are you okay? I say. It takes a minute before she responds, clearly trying to sort through data and figure out what happened, and her heartlight clicks. Mine clicks back. I don't know what happened. I was checking code and maybe I knocked something over: the whole thing just collapsed. I don't know how long we were out, I say.

Does she believe me? I'm not sure.

That's never happened in here before, I say. Do you understand what it might mean? She shakes her head a little. Anyway, it's not important, I don't think. Make your notes as quickly as you can. We need to level out of here if it's gone unstable. As if to echo this, I think I feel a little tremor. It's very slight. Did you feel that? I ask. Her sensors are more finely tuned than mine, but they're not all the way online. Since I trimmed it out she has no memory of what happened just a bit ago and so that gap might disrupt her for some time. She says she didn't feel anything at all. She just looks at me. She asks: Are you okay? You don't look okay.

I wipe away a smear of blood. I'm fine, I say.

Then she asks: What were you doing with the code?

Then she asks: How did the bookshelf collapse?

Then she asks: Is it possible that what you were doing caused the bookshelf to collapse? Could it have caused the tremor?

There's no way I could have caused the tremor. The more I say this the more I start to believe it.

Then she says: I seem to be missing something.

I say: I'm missing something too. I remember the collapse and I remember coming to among the books and you. But I don't know what happened in between.

She says: I seem to be missing something.

I say: Do you want me to clip in to you and run a diagnostic?

She shakes her head.

She says: something's different from when we were here before.

As I turn away I notice another book lit up on the shelf.

I go over to it. I say given what happened to us before I don't think we should spend any more time here than we have to.

She just looks at me.

I say you need to come with me. I say: I need you, Caribou.

I waste no time following the catalyst out.

«

Instead of taking us back to the Christmas scene, the catalyst drops us somewhere else. Same room in a different time. What changed? We're bent over his lap. He is hitting us. I can barely see the room. The pain reverberates. Can't see his face though I turn my head to try. All the detail is on the floor or on the bookshelf where we are facing. There's the book. Next to it is one that takes its title from the egg I planted in the other room. I don't know what to do with that. Things are propagating really fast.

Since I'm the lead I'm the one who's being hit. It doesn't leave me any room for doing anything except receiving blows. Midswing I nod to Caribou and signal her to take a look at the book. She does and says it's blank inside. Then she watches me. Are the others blank inside? I ask. In slow-mo I take a blow. It brings pain but more than pain. It's slow—running at about a 1.5—and so I can actually feel the sensation spread through my body, water coming up over rocks and trickling down, and slowly ebbing so it's just a memory just in time for the next one to come. It's disconcerting, tracking it. I wonder if this is some kind of punishment. *No, it's just this one,* she says.

It hasn't taken long for that egg to propagate. Is that even the metaphor I want? I wonder. I check my clock. We only have a few hours left before the forensics team moves in. We need to be out soon, Caribou says.

I know, I say, as best I can. I'm breathless here. Hand me the book.

She looks at me. It's not a catalyst, she says.

I know, I say. But it wasn't here before. I just want to see it.

I hear the sound of being hit before I feel the smack.

She hands me the book. Father doesn't notice. Father never notices. He can't notice. He's in a loop. We're the only ones with agency in these memories.

I look at the book. It's just a standard cover with the title of the egg. As I open it I see it's filling page by page. I can't read the book. You can't ever read books, because they're not encoded fully. Unless you're a freak you don't remember books word for word. You remember what they were to you, what you brought to them, what you took from them, what you left there of yourself or someone else, maybe. They're here as little smears of memory, vectors and connections, like the role a star plays in a constellation. Sometimes you get a headline or a line from one, the sense of what a chapter might have been like, or a particularly vivid couple of sentences. Any more and it trips a flag. When this book fills in it fills for me. It wouldn't fill for Caribou because she has less subjectivity.

Ever read while being hit? It's hard. So I don't. At best I try to get a little bit of it. For some reason the bits I'm able to make out fill me with sadness. It's like pain recorded. Maybe that's on account of being spanked and being fifteen here, too old, I think for spanking.

Caribou watches as I'm hit again.

I reach back and grip the hairbrush that he's using to spank me with and take the fork.

«

Once I saw the Saudi family's bodies suspended in the operating room as we worked on them. I didn't have clearance to get inside the clean room itself, but everyone could see the tent. They were in the great cavern, the biggest part of the complex on what was once the lowest level. Even now they were digging more below. How low could we go, I wondered, knowing there probably was no answer as long as the money held. It was cold enough already that the jumpsuits we wore had to be upgraded with insulation. So in this big room, maybe a hundred feet across and twenty feet high, there they were, the bodies: up on metallic platforms in what looked like interconnected kiddie pools filled with some kind of gel, all underneath what reminded me of a circus tent in panels of alternately clear and blue. You couldn't see in from outside since the tent had concentric rings with the colors staggered. But if you got up a little, by the supply shop where you had to pick up a transistor package, say, you could see in just enough. There they were, the three primaries, as well as a dozen secondaries. They didn't look like anything, really. They weren't yet dead, though you wouldn't call them alive. They looked like experiments. They weren't nude—instead, they had insisted they must all stay wrapped, no matter what happened. The room inside was clean since any outside influence could affect the chemical mix they would be kept in as long as possible to rip their memories and organize them on the servers. I remember being surprised they were so small. They were the center of everything—we were at the center of everything, the center of the center of this weird country, underneath the surface what must be close to a mile, just off the bluffs that looked out into the sea. It felt like the whole world was concentrated on them at this very moment, as we stripped level after level of data out of them, working against time to make them into—what? homunculi? simulations? frozen libraries of who they thought they were to each other, and thus who they were? I couldn't make sense of it. I felt paralyzed. From my vantage point I could see my way down two of the polished corridors that fed into this room. Because of the way they reflected lights from as far down as you could see before they turned, they looked a little bit like infinity.

Do I even remember that? I know these questions become a loop. How can I trust anything? How can I know I am if I can't know for sure what it is I've done or if I've done or what I've seen. Can I even believe myself to have a self? Yet I do. You have to. How would you go through the world believing you didn't have a self? I know I'm the product of the self-obsessed West, but still I can't get outside myself. I can't see myself. Even in the mirror I can't see myself.

«

We flicker into a hair salon. We're getting our hair done. A man's fingers are running through my hair in little circles, massaging my scalp. There's the exact same hairbrush on the shelf. I'm surprised that the salon would use one too. He's speaking in a voice as low and crisp as a remembered September from my youth, the air bright and cold, trees unleafing for the winter. He's saying nothing in particular. I'm focused only on sensation. Something's awakening in me. I can feel it. This is later the same year. I fixate on the hairbrush: it's exactly like the one I have at home. I've always preferred women's brushes. I like salons. I like scalp massages. These things make me feel like I'm not purely at the mercy of my gender.

«

There are different gradations of real here: when we call a memory real most of us mean true, as in the memory corresponds to the factual record, if there is such a thing. Sometimes what we mean by this is that it can be proved. But we also mean honest or organic: as in we came by the memory honestly, as in it built itself out in our brain without outside influence. We believe it to be true (whether or not it corresponds to fact in this regard is irrelevant). There are lots of ways in which this gets complicated, though: memories are often planted postevent, whether or not they correspond to fact. Ask me whether I remember anecdote X, and with enough specific detail offered by credible sources, I begin to register it dimly. Once it takes hold it can become foundational. Then there are the entirely fake: a section we create wholesale here on the inside postevent. It's easier to copy sections of someone else's memory into a client's brain than it is to rig the thing entire. Sometimes these seem to overwrite other real memories. They don't get erased, not exactly—you can't ever fully erase, because the circuitry's too redundant for that. They get patched and smoothed over and pressed down. Like how when, say, shot with a bullet, the saguaro cactus smooths over the wound and builds up scar tissue over it, incorporating it to continue growing, albeit at a little angle off from how it grew before. Augmented memories get digested and metabolized and narrativized and become part of you too.

So how real are you if you contain augmented memories? How real are we anyway? I think about the I sometimes, that necessary fiction, stretched across all the unstable rest of us like a skin holding in an ocean. It holds us in, mostly, of whatever heterogeneous and unstable stuff we're made. You can't function without it. Even those who lose their memories still know they are an I, a subject. They just don't know exactly who or what they are. But then you do something that you didn't think you'd ever do, and what do you do now? Are you who you were before? Were you just wrong before, or relying on incomplete information? Or are you someone else?

Or Caribou: she now has this little skin inside her, underneath which there's a hole where that memory used to be. Does this make her less a person or companion?

Or the Saudis: Are they still real? They're constructs now but they seem to live. They believe they live. Are they aware just how they live? At least they persist.

Here again is the sensation of fingers moving through my hair and down along my neck. Everything is warm. Here they dip just below the collar of my dress. They penetrate my loneliness just a little. I feel my body tense as if to announce its presence. Then they disappear. I crack my eyes and see that Caribou is looking straight at me as if to see whether I'm enjoying myself. Is it strange to say I am? Is it strange to say how exciting it can be to haunt another's halls? How weird it is to wear another body? I finger the little lighter in my pocket.

With that thought the hands are gone. The room becomes noticeably colder.

«

Caribou signals that we have only an hour to get our asses out of here. I kind of wish she had an ass. Instead, this is an idiom I had added to her programming because I like my girls a little bit profane. Can she be aware of how she's been tweaked? She looks at me as if she does.

«

I run my hand along the memory wall in this event. Here we're back to fire. I smell the fire before I see it. We're here because I simply wanted to see. Here is where the client burned her father's hands and erased a section of his face. Here is where she earns the term *vitrioleuse* after spattering him with acid. This is where her first album title comes from, and it's a great one. You see how she appeared like this: almost fully formed. We see his hand dangling off the side of the huge outdoor tub. I've never seen an outdoor tub before. I figure it must be real. There are two, side by side. It's not a pool. It's obviously a tub, designed for two or more. The air is cool and everything is silent, unusually. We can see the steam rise up and just a bit of his head and feet. Mostly what we feel right now is rage. We are in control, though that's not what she said in court. She said she couldn't remember it, that she was not herself, that she would never do a thing like that. She cried for some time convincingly. I read all the transcripts before coming down. If I'm being honest

I did want to know. It's not my business to pass this judgment along. The charges were dismissed when their history came out, before the forensic techs got in here to assess the situation.

We haven't seen this room before, notes Caribou. Something's off, she says. I'm not sure what, she says.

I can't feel it, I say: this feels right to me. But then I'm in the righteousness so it's hard to separate myself from the role I'm here to play.

Suddenly what I hear is I hear our song, coming from somewhere, first faintly, and as I listen to it, more and more obviously: it's here. It is. It's making its way out. And here I am with the rubber gloves and bucket, trying to move silently through the grass, suddenly listening to this thing singing out of nowhere. I realize it is coming out of me. My lips and breath and body are making it. They're making it as he hears it, too, and turns to see what his daughter's doing, and here I am spattering it all along his body, and here are his screams.

It doesn't take long at all.

I feel no regret for doing it.

I sit a minute after. I feel full of something. Something exciting.

Caribou looks horrified. I didn't realize horror was a feature she could manifest. She's usually better at ignoring emotional content. She's programmed that way. But she looks like she's about to split apart, like something's broken, a bicycle spoke that's deforming a tire as you keep riding on it. I ask her what is happening.

She says: what did you do—without a question mark. It's not a question; it's a remark.

«

I touch the bucket and we backtrack out into another memory. We're on a train: a dining car. I can feel its rhythm, can see the bowed, tandem tracks out the window. We shake a little back and forth. We sway when we walk back and forth. The glasses in the metal cupboards clink. We seem to be going through an industrial area, over and over again. All I see are warehouses out the sides of windows, stacks of pallets, rusting metal walls, a tractor trailer that reads "Cronos" on the side.

This memory is different: it's only Caribou and I in the car. I don't know why we're here. None of the seats are occupied. I gesture to Caribou to sit with me at one of the tables.

She says again: what did you do.

I tell her I didn't do anything.

She says she doesn't believe me.

She asks me what this is. This doesn't look like a memory at all. She says it's made of something else. It's almost full speed, for instance, so it feels like we're moving insanely fast. There's barely enough time to think before I speak. We pass a billboard reading Words Can Hurt. I think it's supposed to be anti-domestic violence or bullying or something of the sort.

I don't know what I'm supposed to say.

Another train comes by, but I can't see in the windows well. It moves too fast; it's more a blur than anything else but it looks empty. All I see is open space inside. We pass a posted sign: "Attention: Remote Control Locomotives Operate in this Area: Locomotive Cars May Be Unoccupied." I don't know what that means.

I start to hear our song again. It's piped in from the tinny speakers in the corners of the car. Caribou says: Is that the same song we heard before? She makes a note. I say that I didn't notice it.

She says: I think we're in trouble here.

She says: I don't see any way out of here.

I don't see a catalyst either.

She says: I don't know where here is or what this has to do with anything.

I realize I'm holding the bucket from the last memory.

We pass a pier from which a ship has just unmoored. It's pouring water from its deck.

I think Caribou knows what I did, I mean, what has occurred.

She says: I can tell you know that song. Where is it from?

I say: I'd never heard it before the last room. I say: Write down the lyrics just in case. We'll check it out when we get out.

We pass into darkness. We must be in a tunnel. The running lights are on, so we can see. She says: We don't have much time. Five minutes now. She says: Do you see a way out for us?

She says: you did something when you put me under. She says: these memories are changed. She says: I read a lot of inconsistencies, and they seem to be growing.

She stares at me.

If this isn't a memory, what is it?

I don't have a response, and I don't know what to do, so I throw the contents of the bucket at her. I don't know what's in it here. It was acid just before.

Now she's wet. She blinks. She says: Why did you do that? She looks entirely flabbergasted: a word I've never before had the opportunity to use. She looks like her world has changed, like she doesn't know who I am anymore.

I can see her calculating, going inward. By now she's determined that she doesn't trust me either. By now she's probably reporting all this back up to management; it might be in the log already. I can't be sure.

Then she starts burning.

She says: I seem to be on fire.

She says: What did you do?

She says: Why don't you help?

She says: What does this mean we are?

To each other? Or at all? I don't say anything. I just stand and watch.

She says: I don't understand.

It doesn't take long until she stops saying anything at all.

What have I done.

Her skin pulls away and soon she stops moving. It seems to take forever for her heartlight to click out. I can't feel mine anymore, but I'm sure it's there.

I'll have to burn the room and hope it disconnects. I have the lighter still from the previous memory. I wonder how. I finger it.

If I can't find a catalyst to bring me back I'll have to fail-safe out. So I touch everything in the car, slowly at first, and then frantically as it starts to dawn on me that there isn't one. The doors don't lead any-where: just to openness, like whatever's out there isn't finished.

I touch the char of Caribou's form on the floor, half-opened as she is. I put my hand on a remaining bit of skin. I slide my finger underneath the seam into her interior. I feel a little like a lover. I'm looking for the nub of flesh that connects her heartlight to her processors. I've never been this close to her. All she is is mesh and lace and wire and bits of sear. This intimacy scares me, even if I know that what she was is gone. She's gone, isn't she? She sure seems gone. I find her nub and hold it, hoping for it to be my catalyst. I'm disappointed that it isn't.

That was the last idea that I had.

Almost as if in response, the song gets a little louder.

I have no choice. I start the curtains in the car on fire. They start to go. Everything's happening so fast it's like I can't control it. Obviously I can't control it. I take a moment to contemplate the fire. It looks pretty good. I can't see the loop. I put my hand in it to see. I look reflexively to Caribou. She doesn't look like Caribou like this. She looks just like a screen. Will she exist when I've fail-safed out? Can she be retrieved? If the room burns after I am gone, all her logs should be erased. There's a decent chance her report won't be recoverable. The story that I'll tell about it later will fit with my history of fire. I'll say it was an accident. I'll say I tried to drag her out. I'll say she malfunctioned there when she touched the fire. They won't care as long as I have the maps, as long as I did my job. Like me, she's replaceable. Will this be a memory the client will have access to? Who knows. I for one don't really care.

The fire's going pretty good now. It's spreading right: the smoke has become a haze, a curtain hanging all across the car. I can't breathe real well, so I get on my knees. The air is cooler here. I put my hands on what used to be Caribou.

I find her input and I enter in the fail-safe code.

For a moment nothing happens. I feel the car shake back and forth. Another train passes without anything or anyone inside.

I enter the code again.

I enter it again.

There is no response, no tearing motion up, no opening, no movement. There's just the rocking of the car, the spreading fire, and the sounds of clinking glass.

I release her nub.

Almost without intention, I slide my hand up to the back of my neck and finger my own seam. I don't know what it means.

Our song continues to play on repeat.

Notes

"Everyone looks better when they're under arrest" was something said by John Waters.

The gnome story was told to me by Page Buono, repeated from someone she'd heard it from, and for some time I assumed it was original, but found out only later that it's a variation on an urban legend. From there it only grew in my mind.

"In a Structure Simulating an Owl" is after a patent, "Structure Simulating an Owl," filed on April 20, 1931, by Grace E. Wilson and granted September 6, 1932.

Acknowledgments

Some of these stories appeared elsewhere, often in substantially different forms:

- "Believing in the Future with the Torturer's Apprentice," in the *Huffington Post*
- "Everyone Looks Better When They're Under Arrest," in *Ploughshares*
- "The Gnome," in *Alta*
- "The Golem," in *Witness*
- "In a Structure Simulating an Owl," in *XO Orpheus: 50 New Myths*
- "It Is Hard Not to Love the Starvationist's Assistant," in *Gulf Coast Online*
- "Opportunities for Intimacy," in *American Short Fiction*
- "This Time with Feeling," in *Harvard Review*
- "Weep No More Over This Event," in *Tin House*

Thanks to those who read and talked about, published, solicited, edited, and/or contributed material to this book: Kate Bernheimer for believing in the Strix; Chris Cokinos for mishearing "Viva Burrito"; Josh Foster for taking on the Starvationist; Paul Hurh for the memorable conversation about the essential sadness of the Pauls; Cheston Knapp for tightening and publishing "Weep No More Over This Event"; Manuel Muñoz and Aurelie Sheehan for their attention to these stories and fellow traveling; and Nicole Walker for Seven Rings and ongoing fellowship (and a little competition). I am glad to be in company with all of you.

164   Particular thanks to Jacqueline Ko and Katie Dublinski for their belief in and shepherding of this book.

It's dark out there/down here. I am particularly grateful to Megan and Athena, my two best co-adventurers, for holding the light.

ANDER MONSON is the author of eight books: four of nonfiction (*Neck Deep and Other Predicaments, Vanishing Point, Letter to a Future Lover,* and *I Will Take the Answer*), two poetry collections (*Vacationland* and *The Available World*), and two books of fiction (*Other Electricities* and *The Gnome Stories*). A finalist for the New York Public Library Young Lions Award (for *Other Electricities*) and a National Book Critics Circle in criticism (for *Vanishing Point*), he is also a recipient of a number of other prizes: a Howard Foundation Fellowship, the Graywolf Press Nonfiction Prize, the Annie Dillard Award for Nonfiction, the Great Lakes Colleges New Writers Award in Nonfiction, and a Guggenheim Fellowship. He edits the magazine *DIAGRAM* (thediagram.com), the New Michigan Press, *Essay Daily* (essaydaily.org), and a series of yearly literary/music tournaments: March Sadness (2016), March Fadness (2017), March Shredness (2018), March Vladness (2019), and March Badness (2020).

The text of *The Gnome Stories* is set in Clerface. Book design by Ann Sudmeier. Composition by Bookmobile Design and Digital Publisher Services, Minneapolis, Minnesota. Manufactured by Sheridan on acid-free, 30 percent postconsumer wastepaper.